Away with the Fairies

Away with the Fairies

MICHAELA TRACEY GARNETT

To order additional copies of this book, contact:
Xlibris Corporation
0-800-644-6988
www.xlibrispublishing.co.uk
Orders@xlibrispublishing.co.uk
302705

Contents

Chapter One

The Little House 11 April 2011

Some time ago—I'm not sure how long, but it was some time ago—there lived a young girl named Poppy, who was named after the poppy fields that grew when her grandfather had died whilst proudly fighting for his country.

Poppy was often lonely. Her only friend in the world was her grandmother. They lived alone in a little village at number 12, Lacigam Drive.

Poppy wasn't really like other children. She wasn't special, and she didn't have any talent that separated her from other children in her class. At the age of thirteen, she liked to read, write, and learn. All the other girls her age weren't bothered in school; they would chat and text under the table. Poppy didn't even have a phone. Maybe the way she had been brought up with her grandmother's old traditions and Christian beliefs put a block on Poppy's social life.

Although Poppy loved to learn, she was very easily distracted. 'You're away with the fairies again!' was often said to her by her grandmother or teachers. Seldom did she hear them; she was too busy lost in her magical worlds inside the pages of the books she would often read over and over again.

'Can I go and play in the gardens, Grandma?' asked Poppy, lifting her head from the pages of a book.

'Bored of that book already, Poppy? Of course, you can! What's the rule?' Smiled her grandmother, kindly.

Poppy jumped from her grandmother's floral printed armchair's grasp and ran through the back door leading to the gardens.

'Don't go past the trees!' she shouted as she reached the fresh summer's air, her voice trailing behind her.

Her grandmother chuckled. 'Away with the fairies again!' She laughed, shaking her head and relaxing into the chair, closing her eyes as she listened to the peaceful quietness of her home.

Poppy sat on the grass, making daisy chains. It was the middle of summer, and daisies were in full bloom. They always seemed to grow bigger and brighter in her grandmother's big garden. Poppy was happiest at this time of year as there was no learning to do. Poppy was away from the glare of her friends, and the hiss of their whispers was behind her back. She was free to do whatever she liked, the way she liked it, without anyone to judge her. Humming a nursery rhyme to herself in her sweet voice, she caught sight of the line of tall, evergreen trees that looked like Christmas trees her grandmother had always told her not to venture past. Poppy felt a surge of excitement burst through her; it was like something, a magnet, hidden in the depths of the leaves, was pulling her to the branches and beyond. Guessing the time, she assumed she had a couple of hours until it went dark and had to go inside, so she quickly checked her grandmother wasn't looking and dared to disappear into the branches of the line of the forbidden trees.

As she ran through the forest, feeling the wind in the hair, her heart burning wild with excitement, she felt so brave and free. She outstretched her arms and let the branches of the trees weave their way through her fingers quickly. Suddenly, she stopped at a bridge. It looked old, and the wood it was made from was rotting slightly at the side and part of it was hidden in moss. She took in a deep breath, and her new, overpowering, daring streak overcame her, and she ran across fast. A huge sigh left her mouth as she reached solid ground on the other side. She picked up her pace and started to run again, looking up at the sun peeping through the branches of the trees.

Suddenly, the ground went from beneath her, and she fell down, hitting the ground and rolling down through shrubs and dirt. She tried not to shout as she fell, not wanting to alert her grandmother. She stood up and winced in pain, a few cuts on her arm from the branches but nothing serious. Poppy stood up and brushed the dirt from her dress. She was in complete wilderness; the path she was following was completely out of sight. The trees in front of her seemed knitted tight together; there was no way to get past those. Now she knew why she couldn't pass the trees. Now she wished she didn't.

She turned around to climb the small hill she fell down as she raised her arm to grab the long branch trailing down the side in order to hoist herself up.

'No stupid!' came a whispered voice from behind her.

Poppy froze.

'Hello?' she said into the trees. Suddenly, she wasn't so excited to be wandering around the forest behind her grandmother's house alone.

She turned around slowly and saw the same as she had seen before, except a big willow tree in the corner of her eye. It looked as if a tall someone was hunched over, head bent with his or her knotted grey hair sweeping the ground. She was certain it wasn't there before. *It would've gone unmissed?*

'I said get rid of the trees! Not put more in!' the same voice whispered again, scornfully.

'Hello?' Again Poppy got no reply. Her heart was racing; her breath was, too.

She shook her head and told herself she must have heard the wind in her ears, although she didn't believe herself. She turned again and began to climb the branches on the small, steep hill.

'Good! You finally did it right for once!' said the voice again, louder.

It's nothing, Poppy! Ignore it and run all the way home!

It was too late; the branches of the bushes faded beneath her and soon were gone. Poppy found she was holding on to thin air and fell backwards on to her back, back down into the wilderness.

Did I just hear a door close?

But there was no wilderness. When Poppy picked herself up again, she found all the trees and shrubs had completely disappeared. In their place, there was a little wooden house with a thatched roof and flowers overflowing prettily in the window box. It was just like the pictures she had seen in the fairytale books she'd read. She stared for some seconds in awe of the little house and blinked hard a couple of times.

Surely I'm dreaming?

Pinching her arm didn't wake her up. Poppy felt her daring streak return and then slowly gathered up the courage to tap gently on the perfect wooden door at the front of the house. Clenching her fist, she stood staring up at the house, waiting for an answer, a shout, a movement, or anything that showed there was someone or something inside. After waiting for what seemed like hours, she moved away and started to circle the house.

After walking the pebble path around the house about three times, putting each foot toe to heel and putting out her arms to balance herself, each time she was taking in a different part of the house, the patterns in wooden frame of the windows, the slight cracks in the light, pink-coloured outer walls of the house, and the colours of the pebbles in the path that led to a circle around the house.

I wonder the point of this path; all it does is circle the house, maybe just to look nice. I can't imagine anyone wanting to walk the path unless they are bored like me. It leads to nowhere and isn't very long, maybe it is for decoration.

Her trail of thoughts carried on and on for a while until she started to get dizzy and decided to sit down outside the front door, deciding it'd be rude to just walk in and so to wait for the occupant of this wonderful house to return home.

She caught sight of a patch of daisies, not far from the house and searched in her dress pocket for the daisy chain she made earlier and went across to complete her daisy necklace with the patch of daisies. These daisies looked even better than the ones in her grandmother's garden; they didn't even look real, like something that popped out of a fairytale along with the house. She decided that if the person or creature that lived in the house was kind enough to let her in, she would give them the daisy chain to hang on the door for decoration.

After completing the daisy chain, she began to get bored of waiting for whoever lived in the house to return. She lay in the sun, closed her eyes, and listened to the busy silence of the forest, the tweeting birds; soft breeze and running water were like a lullaby, and Poppy drifted into a soft sleep. Her dreams of living in the little house with her grandmother and reading all the fairytale books in the sunny garden were so vivid that she was shocked when she awoke to hear her grandmother frantically shouting her name. She jumped up and realised she wasn't meant to be in this part of the forest and dropped the daisy chain that was on her lap. She ran and put it in front of the door so whoever lived there could find it when they returned home. *What if they had returned? Maybe they came home and left her to sleep in the sun?* She raised her hand to knock again when her name was shouted across the forest by her grandmother. She ran from the house and, back up the little bank she slid down on her way there, ran across the little bridge over the river that ran through to the other side of the forest and through the trees and followed her grandmother's voice to her garden where she stood with a worried look plastered on her face.

'Where on earth have you been? I've been shouting you!' cried her grandmother as she approached her.

'I'm sorry. I fell asleep by the river, Grandma,' she replied, hanging her head.

'It's okay. Dinner's ready. Come on inside before it gets cold!'

They went inside the back door of her grandmother's modernized black-and-white cottage and sat down at the large table that could probably seat about five people but was only set for two with glasses of pomegranate juice, Grandma's favourite, and chicken and vegetables with gravy in a floral jug in the middle of the table.

'Grandma, do you know what is past those trees in the forest?' Poppy asked excitedly as they tucked into their dinner.

'Well, I hear there is the river and a bit of a steep bank, and well, there isn't much else really,' she replied before concentrating on cutting her chicken.

'Really? Then why aren't I allowed past them?'

Her grandmother took especially long to chew the carrots she put in her mouth as if thinking of some sort of excuse, and after a short silence, her grandmother replied, 'The bank, it's very steep. You could hurt yourself or fall. Please promise me you won't go past those trees, Poppy. I don't want you to hurt yourself.'

I already have hurt myself, Grandma!

Poppy slid her hand under the table and crossed over her fingers and nodded her head.

'I promise.'

Poppy frowned as she looked down at her food, barely touched. *What has come over her?*

She always did as she was told. She was always honest. Not anymore.

She was breaking rules, promises, and what's more, her grandmother's trust.

Chapter Two

Disobeying Grandma

The next morning, Poppy dressed herself in her best yellow, summer dress and went into the garden to play where her grandmother was planting some elegant white roses in the flowerbeds. On the table was a little tray of iced cakes her grandma had made the previous day. She took one for herself and hid one in her dress pocket; this one was for the owner of the house. Poppy imagined a kind old lady to live there that baked cakes just like her grandmother and sewed little cushion covers for her sofa inside her home and planted seeds that would soon grow into beautiful roses in front of her garden. She imagined the woman would open the door with a smile on her face and invite her in, and they would chat all afternoon, eating biscuits and drinking tea. Maybe she would like to meet Grandma; they could bake together and join in her tea parties with the old woman. Or maybe they already knew each other, but they weren't friends, that's why they split the forest, and Poppy wasn't allowed to go through to the other side because her grandmother didn't want her meeting the lady she didn't like.

Whichever it was, whoever it was, Poppy was determined to find out. She kissed her grandmother on the cheek and skipped into the forest and sat down in the grass where she was making daisy chains yesterday and sang to herself. She was well in sight of her grandmother, so stayed there for a while until her grandmother went inside. Then she would run through the branches, over the bridge, and down the bank and to the house with the old woman she dreamed of being there.

As she approached the house, it looked just as beautiful as it had the day before; the plants were still in the window box, and the pebbled path was still intact; everything was perfect. She edged closer to the house and stood still at the door as she reached upwards to knock on the door. She saw the daisy chain she had made was withered and dull looking and hadn't been moved. *Maybe the person that lived in the house didn't notice the daisies she had left there because they were in a rush when they got home, or maybe they thought they looked too pretty to move?* Poppy had so many questions to ask the person that lived here: why they lived here, why they don't leave that part of the forest—which she didn't think they did because she had never seen a stranger near Grandma's house—why have they never visited Grandma? and why didn't they pick up the daisies?

Eagerly, she knocked on the door of the little house and waited again for what seemed like hours, but again, there was no reply. She followed the path round the house until she came to a window and peered through it. The glass was very dusty from inside, and it was difficult to see inside. *How could they be out again? Or did they even return from yesterday?* So many more questions were building up inside of Poppy, and the more there were, the more determined she was to find out.

'Just do it quick before she comes back!' whispered the same voice from yesterday.

Poppy jumped in her skin as she heard footsteps; more than one pair of feet ran across the inside of the house, and then a door was heard closing.

I was NOT imagining that! Who is that?

She turned slowly and tiptoed round to the front where the door had been opened just about an inch. The hair on the back of Poppy's neck stood up and sent a shiver down her spine.

'Is anyone there?' shouted Poppy into the house.

Of course, there was no reply on the front door, and surprisingly, it opened. She told herself to remember to tell whoever lived there to be more responsible when they go out because anyone could have just walked in.

She pushed open the door but stood glued in her spot. She craned her neck to look inside, but it was too dark to see anything, so she took a deep breath and took a step inside. She stood in shock at the sight before her; it was nothing like she had dreamed or imagined of. In fact, it was the complete opposite.

The house was completely desolate. There were dust and cobwebs all over everywhere. There wasn't much furniture, just a table and a couple of chairs in the middle of the first room, which she dare not sit on because it looked so old it would snap and fall, and an old-looking bookcase. She moved her head slowly to gaze around the room and saw a door on one side; slowly she walked through the dirty room and turned the handle on the door.

Brushing the dust off her hand on her dress, she stared at the horror in this room just like she had done the last. It was an empty room, small, almost like a room that would be used as a bedroom; there wasn't much to see, and so closing the door behind her, she made her way back to the main room, where she saw another door, opposite the one she had just entered.

She entered the new room. It was also small with strangely just one single book lying on the floor. She bent down and brushed the dust off it, and looking at the cover, she read the words *fairies* on the front. She put it into her dress pocket, but it wouldn't fit without her taking out the cake. She felt dirty eating it in this environment, so she held it in her hand as she left the room. She'd been everywhere in the house. *Where had those footsteps she heard ran to?* The thought of something being in the house with her made her shiver although she wanted to know what was in this mysterious book. So she placed the cake down on the table and opened the book.

As she did this, she heard her grandmother shout her name. She slammed it shut, shoved it in her pocket, and ran towards the front door, closing it carefully. She ran for the bank as fast as she could. It was obvious to her now that no old lady that liked to bake and sew and have tea parties lived here. She now knew the meaning of 'Don't judge a book by its cover.' Because the outside of this house led her to believe a fairytale, while its inside was a horror.

Chapter Three

Book of Wonder

Finally she was alone. All afternoon she was helping Grandma with the chores: she helped make dinner, set the table, helped her grandmother put out the washing, ate dinner, and washed up. Now finally, she could sit in peace and read the book she had found. She studied the front cover. It was a pink, hardbacked book with the word *fairies* printed across the front cover. There was a rough drawing of a fairy and some glitter here and there, but other than that, the cover was plain. She turned the book in her hands and saw that the back of the book had something scrawled on it in pen. It was scratched and dirty, but she could make out the words *for my darling,*' and then there were some more dirt and scratches like *have fun drawing*, *your birthday*, *love, Mum and Dad*. The rest was hard to read and had worn away, but she guessed it was a present for whoever had lived there in the house from her parents.

What's happening to you, Poppy? Now you're stealing!

Poppy shook her head as if to shake away the thoughts in her head. She opened the book carefully. The first page had *My Fairy Book* scrawled across it in what looked like a child's handwriting. She turned the page with caution and saw a beautiful drawing of a fairy queen across the page. Her dress was long and flowing and had every colour possible splashed over it in little curls. She was stunning with emerald green eyes, deep, pink, shiny lips, and a sparkling golden crown balanced on her long, dark curls down to her waist. Poppy let her fingers run over her hair on the page. She imagined it to be soft and bouncy and flow in the wind when she flew with her glittering pair of wings. Around her neck hung a wonderful golden necklace covered in lots of jewels. She studied the fairy queen's dress and realised that there was a little caption at the bottom saying 'Fairy queen of Dreamland—Karena' in black ink.

She found it hard to draw her eyes away from such realistic face. There was no way the child who owned the book drew this. It was like someone had taken a photo of her although she was certain fairies didn't exist and neither did such beauty. After a while of staring at the perfectness of the drawing, she turned the page slowly and gently as if the fairy was so delicate it could feel the page turning beneath her.

On the next page was a male fairy. He stood broad with dark hair and a handsome face; his brown eyes seemed to be staring straight at Poppy, into her mind, into her thoughts. He wore white trousers and a blue shirt over his delicate-looking wings with high, black boots and again wore a golden crown on his head. The caption underneath said 'Prince Alexander.' Again, she couldn't take her eyes off him, but this time, it wasn't because it was his looks that kept her there, it was almost as if she was possessed by him. She wanted to move and turn the page, but she couldn't. She felt like she had lost all control of her body. His eyes seemed to be burning into her.

She turned the page again gently and saw a young girl. This time, a tiara or a crown was missing from her head, but she had, like the others, exceptional beauty, which was unlike the fairy queen but a unique beauty. Her hair was very light, almost white, and was bone straight down to her chin and curved perfectly around her face; she wore a yellow pinafore dress and had wonderful colourful wings although not as big as the royal fairies. She had a kind face and bright blue eyes like the sky on a sunny day. The caption read 'My best friend—Yasmina.'

Again, she studied the pencil line on the page and wondered how just a small stick of lead could create such beauty and wished from so deep in her heart she could have so much beauty as these fairies did. As she turned the page, she almost dropped the book in horror. There was a young girl stood in a blue and white spotted dress and a matching hairband, this time with no wing and tiara. The girl on the page staring at Poppy *was* Poppy. She looked exactly like her. Poppy grabbed her dressing table mirror and, after examining the picture, she examined her own face, the pointed, ski-slope nose, the thick slightly pouted lips, the green-blue eyes, and the blonde hair, which on this little girl was tied in plaits. Every single feature was a replica. Poppy searched for the caption. This time reading 'Me.' *How could whoever had drawn in this book look exactly like Poppy?* She knew she didn't draw it herself because she didn't have the best drawing skills and didn't remember.

The door opened, and Poppy's Grandmother entered with a start. She caught sight of Poppy who had hardly noticed her enter and was mesmerized in the book. 'Where did you find that?' she insisted, snatching it out of Poppy's hands.

'I I,' she stuttered.

'WHERE Poppy?' she shouted angrily.

'I'm sorry, Grandma! I went past the trees. I'm sorry. I was looking for more daisies,' she lied.

'What did you see? Where did you get this?' Grandma questioned, trying to be calm as she could see she was frightening Poppy.

'I found a little house. I waited for the owner to come home, but they didn't, so I went inside. I wasn't nosy. I just had a little look around, and then I found this book. I don't think anyone lived there. It was empty and dirty, Grandma. I was going to give the book back. I just wanted a look in it. The pictures are beautiful. Have a look, Grandma! Just in case anyone did live there, I left a cake on the table!' she insisted.

'How could you have possibly found the house? And well, that will be gone tomorrow. You shouldn't have disobeyed me, Poppy, and you shouldn't have taken this,' she said, holding out the book.

'What will be gone tomorrow?'

'The cake!'

'Why?'

'The fair . . . the animals, there are animals in the forest. They would eat it.'

'Oh, I know. I'm sorry, Grandma. I truly am. Please come with me to return the book.'

'No, it's too late, and this book belonged to your mother, so we can't return it. Not ever.'

'My mother's? What's it doing in someone's house? Did she draw those pictures, grandma? Have you seen them? They are stunning!'

'Yes, I've seen them. I can still see them now. Your mother would sit for hours drawing in her little house. I never saw her. She became obsessed with her imaginary fairies. Your grandfather built her the house when she was young, so she had somewhere to play in the forest, but soon she started telling us of the fairy friends she made in the forest. At first, I thought she just had a vivid imagination. She had a great talent of drawing, she would draw on anything she could find, and so her father and I made her this book so she could keep her drawings together. Her drawing was so realistic. I honestly thought she was seeing things when she told me she had drawn real fairies. So one day, I followed her into her little house and watched from the window as she pulled back a bookshelf revealing a door. She took a key from inside one of the books and opened the door. A bright light shone through it, and she stepped inside. Concerned of where she was going, I followed her at a distance, and sure enough, we had entered another land I suppose. The weather was brilliant, and fairies flew about here and there. I stood amazed and watched my daughter play around and laugh with things I thought *didn't exist.*'

There was a long pause as Poppy took in the story her grandmother had just reeled off to her. 'Wow! What happened then?'

'I never questioned her about it. I just left and waited for her to return home, and she didn't say anything at dinner. She had always thought I just thought she was making it all up in her head. But of course, years on, the time came for your mother to grow up and start her life, so she said goodbye to the fairies and began her new job and married your father. Soon after you were born, they divorced. She always spoke of how she wouldn't want you to go to see the fairies as she wouldn't want you to be labelled as mad for believing in them, and then when she died, the little house was neglected, and I don't want to go inside. I know if

I do, I will go searching for the door and enter the fairy world and get attached like your mother did. Instead, I just planted trees all around it in a hope to hide it. I don't have the heart to knock it down, Poppy.' Poppy's grandmother took out a handkerchief from her skirt pocket and wiped the tears rolling down her face.

'So that's why. That's why the picture of the girl looks exactly like me. It wasn't me, and it was my mother. What should we do now, Grandma?'

'I'll keep this book. Thank you for rescuing it for me. Now you MUST promise me you won't go looking for the fairy world, Poppy, and you MUST not go back to that house so long as I'm here. Okay?'

'Yes, Grandma.'

That night, Poppy lay in bed, and every time she closed her eyes, she saw the prince staring straight back at her. At first, this scared her, but she soon came to let them comfort her. When she fell asleep, she dreamed she saw the prince, he started to speak to her, and his voice was soft, heart-warming, loving, and everything a kind, handsome prince's voice should be. Strangely, he was holding the cake she had left on the table as he began to speak. He didn't say much, just, 'Come to us. Come, Poppy, find us.' Poppy wasn't sure if this meant anything, but she had promised her grandmother she wouldn't go back. She didn't know what to do.

After debating whether to obey her grandmother or the fairy prince, she decided the handsome prince dream was just her imagination and the fairies didn't even know she existed.

Every night for many weeks, Poppy had the same dream, the same eyes burning into her mind, the same voice, pleading with her to come and find him.

Chapter Four

The Note

Poppy lay on her bed and kicked off her party shoes. She had just returned from her fourteenth birthday party. Her grandmother invited all the neighbours around and a few of her grandmother's bingo friends, and they ate lots of party food like sausages and little bits of cheese and mini onion on a cocktail stick and lots of birthday cake. Her stomach felt heavy and her feet ached. Although it wasn't the party she always dreamed, Poppy loved her grandma for making such an effort. She had stuck banners and blown up balloons everywhere in the lounge and kitchen whilst she sent Poppy to the shops and then shouted 'Surprise!' holding a big, chocolate cake when she walked in, with fourteen lit pink candles on top, whilst the other guests threw streamers and blew little party whistles—the kind that when you blew into them, a piece of ribbon would uncurl and a short sound would be emitted. Poppy giggled as she remembered Norman, her grandmother's neighbour, telling Poppy how she was going to have great adventures in far-off lands.

What a silly man! She thought. *Everyone knows I'm going to stay here and teach at the local school!*

She knew exactly what would happen once she fell asleep and began to curl up. She had become very fond of this dream; the eyes and the voice of the prince made her feel happy and safe. It's just his pleads that she wished she could do something about.

'Grandma?'

Poppy knocked on her grandma's door. She was normally up by 8 a.m., but now it was 10 a.m., and Poppy couldn't see why she would be so tired to sleep in late.

She pushed open the door and walked towards the window where she opened the curtains to let light into the dark room. 'Come on, Grandma. You can't stay in bed all day!'

As she turned from the window towards her grandmother's bed, she let out a little scream as she saw her grandmother lay stiff, clutching the fairy book. She knew as soon as she saw her grandmother that she was dead.

Through tear-filled eyes, Poppy gazed at her somehow peaceful grandmother; she seemed to have a soft look in her face and a slight smile. Poppy shook her arm.

'Wake up,' she whispered.

'Grandma, wake up!' She knew she was dead, but she had to try and wake her up.

She was almost hysterical; she shook her grandmother's arm rather violently.

'GRANDMA, WAKE UP. PLEASE! GRANDMA!'

No, no! This can't be happening!

She had never seen a dead person before, but her grandmother's body didn't frighten her.

'Oh Grandma, what am I to do without you?' is all she could force out of her quivering mouth as she fell to the floor next to the bed and wept.

'I'm so sorry. I disobeyed you, Grandma! I'm so sorry. I lied! Please come back!'

Poppy clasped her hands and looked up to the ceiling; she did just how her grandmother had taught her. She said god was always willing to forgive one's sins.

Please god! Bring back my grandma! I'm so sorry I broke her rules. I'm so sorry I disobeyed. I promise I will be good. I'll do all my work and do everything that's asked of me, and I'll tidy my room, and and . . . She isn't going to come back, is she, god? Why did you take her from me, god? Why? Do you need another angel that badly?

Poppy gave up on her prayers; she was starting to get hysterical again. She cried even harder.

She closed her eyes tighter and tighter. They started to hurt, but Poppy didn't care. She continued to squeeze her eyes tighter, praying that when she opened them that her grandmother would be alive and well and ask why Poppy was crying, but of course, when Poppy opened her eyes, her grandmother was still dead.

She wept for a while, but all the while, she had her eyes closed. She could see the fairy prince. He seemed to comfort her and make her happier; his eyes filled Poppy with warmth and calmed her down. Poppy looked up to the bed where her grandmother lay still and thought hard about what to do. She didn't know whom to call and whom to go to.

She was clueless. She felt like crying again, but she caught sight of the book in her grandmother's hands. Carefully, she prised it away from her grandmother's cold hands that were still soft. Sadness overwhelmed her as she realised that her grandmother was, without a doubt, lay there dead. As she lifted the book, a little envelope fell out of the pages.

Poppy bent down to pick up the envelope. She saw that in her grandmother's handwriting was written 'To my darling, Poppy.'

She carefully opened the envelope and sat on the floor as she began to read.

Dear Poppy,

    I'm sorry to have left you like I have, and I hope you are not too scared or frightened about finding me. I was so happy that you found this book; I have been looking for it everywhere for years after your mother died, and now I know the book is safe. I can pass on and join your mother and grandfather. I know I made you promise Poppy, but go. Go to the house, and go to the fairies. Tell them about the house, the book, me, your mother, and this letter. Pack up your things and the fairies will help you refurnish your mother's little house. Live there and with the fairies, they will look after you.

    Goodbye, Poppy. Take good care of this book, the fairies, and yourself. Don't ever return to the real world after entering the fairy world, and don't do anything about me. I will be looked after. Just leave the house now, and don't ever come back.

I love you, Poppy.
Grandma.'

Poppy's eyes were filled with tears as she stood up and looked at her grandmother for a while, knowing she would never see her again. She bent down, hesitated, and carefully kissed her grandmother's cheek. Her flesh to Poppy's lips felt horrible and cold, but Poppy was happy she did it.

Suddenly, her grandmother's whole body began to glisten. Then, just like the trees in the forest, she faded away and disappeared.

She went to leave the room, and as she turned, she whispered, 'I love you too, Grandma.'

Chapter Five

Leaving

Poppy climbed on her desk and retrieved her rucksack from the top of her wardrobe, and through tears, she folded the letter and put it into her pocket and quickly packed her clothes and other important things like her party make-up (just in case!) and her favourite fairytale book, including her mother's picture into the bag and left her room. She went into her grandmother's room, half expecting to see her grandmother walking around, but of course, she wasn't. She went over to her dressing table and picked up the little, silver teddy bear necklace and tied it round her neck so she would always have her grandmother with her. On the way out, she noticed a picture of her grandma and mother on holiday when her mother was younger, and she grabbed the framed picture and put it into her bag and started off on her adventure.

There it was again—the picturesque, fairytale house she had looked upon before. Without hesitation, she entered the house and began the search for a bookcase. Before long, she found the bookcase in the far corner of the room she first entered last time. It took a while and most of Poppy's strength, but she moved the bookcase, revealing a door. Poppy's hands were shaking as she reached for the handle and turned it.

It was locked. Poppy had no idea where she was supposed to find the key, and after trying for ages to open the door, she sat in the middle of the floor and began to cry. Suddenly, she had a thought. *Maybe the prince can help!*

She closed her eyes tight and waited for him to appear. He didn't say anything. He just stared lovingly into her eyes, again filling Poppy with warmth and happiness.

But it wasn't enough this time to make everything okay. Poppy had to find the key; without it, she couldn't enter the fairy world, and she would be stuck forever.

The prince's mouth began to open, and when the sound came out, his voice echoed in Poppy's mind, 'Books.'

Then he disappeared. Poppy sat in a state of confusion.

She had no idea what 'books' meant, but she had to find out. She went over to the bookshelf. There were not many books on the shelves, and the ones that were there weren't interesting or what Poppy felt was relative to the situation.

She picked up *Birds of the Forest* and flicked through the pages; as she did this, it triggered in her mind when her grandmother was telling her a story. She got the key from inside one of the books. She franticly began flicking through the books' pages, throwing them on the floor; as she did, finally, in a very dusty book hidden at the back called *Fairytales for Girls,* the key dropped out of the pages and dropped on to the floor.

She held the key in her shaking hands and inserted it into the lock and began to turn it. It was just as her grandmother had described, and a blinding white light shone into her face. Through squinted eyes, Poppy stepped through the door and into a dreamland.

Chapter Six

Familiar Faces

Poppy couldn't believe it. There, stood before her, was the fairy queen in all her glory, her kind, emerald eyes, her long, brown hair, and her glittering, stunning dress. It was like she had stepped off the pages of her book. The handsome fairy prince, again, looked exactly like he did in the book and in her dreams; his beautiful eyes stared into her lovingly. She rubbed her eyes with her hands, she pinched her arm, she tried everything, and she assumed she looked so silly in front of them, waiting for her to react, but she couldn't wake herself up from this dream. That's when it hit her. This wasn't a dream.

She looked around her. The sun was shining defiantly; there wasn't a cloud in the brilliant, bright blue sky. In the distance, she could see fairies flying about here and there, but to her surprise, they weren't tiny little creatures whizzing around with gold dust following at their feet; they were normal, human size. They looked like normal humans, apart from the fact their feet weren't on the floor and they had wings on their backs. Each one had beauty defined; they were dressed in fine clothes, and all had glistening hair. They seemed to have exceptional beauty—a beauty some would not believe possible if they had not seen it themselves.

Poppy opened her mouth to speak, but she was so shocked she couldn't get any words out.

She closed her mouth and then opened it again but still nothing. After many attempts, she realised she must look a bit like a goldfish so forced out a little 'ngh.' She had no idea what it meant, but still it was a sound.

'Hello, Poppy dear, welcome to the land of the fairies. Your mother told you about us I believe,' spoke the queen in a soft and caring voice.

'Um, I. Poppy couldn't concentrate; her eyes were fixed to the fairy prince, and his were to her.

'Poppy?' the queen questioned.

'Um, no, she kept it a secret. She said she didn't want me to be "labelled as mad for believing in them" when I make a start in life, so my grandma told me. She told me about the fairy world, and she told me to come here in this note when she died.' She got out the little note from her pocket and handed it to her.

The fairy prince spoke up after realising he had been gazing at Poppy for so long he had forgotten to introduce himself.

'Ah, so why didn't you follow my calls? I came to you every night in your dreams. Sometimes I was there when you closed your eyes. Why didn't you come?'

'My grandma, she told me to stay away. She made me promise never to return to my mother's little house, but when she died, she left me this note. She knew she was going to die, so she told me to come here, and you will look after me. She told me I must live in my mother's house and never return the real world. Now I have seen you,' she said, stopping herself from swooning in shock at the prince's voice, exactly like the ones in her dreams. He even wore the same clothes, and he even had the same smile. She knew that from this point, she was in love with a prince. *How silly!*

'Yes, you must live here now. Let's go into the house, and I will use my magic to restore it into a home for you, Poppy, and tomorrow, you will meet the other fairies,' spoke the queen, getting out a long golden stick that seemed to sparkle in the sunlight before they started walking through the trees and suddenly back through the door into her house.

Chapter Seven

A New Life

Poppy woke from a deep sleep and sat up in her new bed. That was the first time in months she hadn't seen the fairy prince in her dreams. She looked around the new room the fairy queen's spell had made for her: her lovely wooden dressing table and stool that had flowers and swirls engraved on to the pine; the many pictures of her and her mother and grandmother and grandfather all in a thin silver frame on the walls; her little wooden wardrobe, matching the dressing table; and her bed with a white and pink duvet, the comfiest one she had ever slept in! She soon realised that everything that happened yesterday wasn't a dream. It really was real! Suddenly, sadness hit her as she would never see her grandmother again. She would never help set the table, never run through the forest to meet her grandmother's worried calls, never dress in her Sunday best to go to church with Grandma, never bake the special pink cakes she and her grandmother made together, and never take for granted all the little things she knew she was going to miss ever again. She had lost everyone, and although she had all her new stuff around her, she felt she had lost everything.

After getting dressed, she went through to the middle section of the house, the one that she saw it before was dusty and old, and it was now bright and clean. Again, there were pictures all over the walls, the way she liked it. The old table and chairs had been replaced with a new one, and around it was a kitchen sink, a stove, and some cupboards.

In the other half of the room was the bookcase—all new and full of books she liked to read, including her mother's book of drawings and a new, big golden one, containing the key to the door behind the bookcase—and a lovely big flowery printed armchair and cushions for her to relax and read on.

She entered the room opposite her bedroom, the one where she found her mother's book, and saw a desk and a chair in there, lots of different material lay around on shelves and in the corner of the room. In the draws of the desk were sewing kits and wool and thread. Poppy had already decided last night that she would help the fairies by making them clothes because they have helped her so much. She already knew how to sew because her grandmother had taught her.

She left the room and ate a banana from her new fruit bowl for breakfast and then went over to the bookcase. Carefully, she shifted it over to reveal the door and looked for a while and thought, *I don't need to hide the door anymore.* So she left the bookcase where it was, took out the key, and entered the fairy world.

Chapter Eight

New Friends

She stepped out of the trees, closing the door behind her and into a little town.

Poppy had slept one night and felt like she had fallen asleep as a thirteen-year-old and woken up years older. She felt new, mature, and grown up.

Fairies flew here and there into houses and little shops. They all stood opposite each other in a long line and a cobbled path led in-between them and led up to a huge palace in the distance. She assumed this was the fairy queen's.

Poppy had a few coins in her pocket, so she thought she would buy some flowers to plant outside her house and some fruits for her kitchen. She would also put up some posters here and there, advertising her dress making. She needed to make a living after all; she couldn't believe she was only just fourteen and already she had to act like an adult. Poppy loved the warmness of the sun as she skipped down the road. Surprisingly, all the fairies knew her name and smiled and said hello as they flew past her.

Wow! It's almost I have the thing I've always wanted. Friends!

She passed bakers, and the smell of fresh bread floated in the air, and Poppy took a deep breath, inhaling the smell. She passed hairdressers where she could see fairies getting a new 'do' through the big glass windows. She saw the station where fairies were being greeted by family and friends as they stepped off the old-fashioned steam trains. Finally, after passing many other homes and shops, one including a school where the laughter of children filled the air, she came to a florist; inside was a beauty. She saw different kinds of flowers, roses, tulips, poppies, daffodils, sunflowers, marigolds, orchids, and lilies. She gazed at them all in amazement. She wanted to take them all home with her. They all stood in their own beauty, but she could only afford one, so she took out a bunch of poppies, thinking they were perfect for her house because of the name and went to the counter to pay where a little girl with beautiful blue eyes and blonde ringlet hair sat, swinging her legs and drawing on a piece of paper.

'Hello, there! Surely you can't be selling me flowers, little girl?' asked Poppy kindly.

'No, I'm watching out for customers whilst Mummy makes bouquets. I'm Amelia. Nice to meet you!' said the little girl in a sweet voice.

'Aw, hello, Amelia, that was my mummy's name you know. I'm Poppy!'

'I know who you are. Everyone knows you. You're the great Amelia's daughter and have come to help us and live with us!' she said.

'Oh, yes, did the fairy queen tell you?'

'Yes. And the fairy prince. They told everyone!'

'Okay, may I speak to your mummy please?'

The little girl ran into the back and out came a tall, pretty woman. She had a short, light blonde bob that curved around her face. It took Poppy a few minutes to realise, but this woman was the third fairy in the book!

'Hello, Poppy, hope Amelia didn't annoy you too much. I'm.—'

'Yasmina. Your name is Yasmina.'

The woman didn't look shocked at all. She just smiled.

'Ah, I see you found your mother's book then! It only seems yesterday we sat here in my mother's shop as she drew me.'

Poppy smiled as Yasmina reminisced and spoke.

'Amelia is a very sweet girl!'

'I should hope. She is named after your mother!'

'Really? Wow!'

'Yes, she was my best friend. I was devastated when she left us,' she whispered softly. Poppy could hear her heartbreak in her voice so tried to change the conversation.

'Please can I pay for these?'

'Oh, you can have those for free this time! I hope to see you soon, Poppy!'

'And you too! Oh, before I go, please can you put one of these up in your shop?' She handed over the small poster she had made, advertising her dress making

'Of course. See you soon, Poppy!'

'Thank you! Bye, Yasmina, Bye, Amelia!'

She shouted to the little girl as she left the shop and carried on to the little fruit and vegetable shop.

* * *

Placing the apples in the bowl, she grabbed her gardening gloves, put on her coat, and headed outside to plant her flowers. As she opened the door, she caught sight of the forest she once played in and the journey she would make to get back to her grandmother's house. She wanted more than anything to go back there and see her grandmother waiting for her. She wanted to hear her grandma shouting her with a worried tone of voice with dinner on the table, but she remembered the letter. She mustn't go back, so she didn't. She had to obey her grandmother wherever she was.

She planted the flowers in the window boxes, and it looked itself again, the little house, right off the pages of her fairytale books.

She headed inside and put away her gloves and began to look through her mother's book as she heard a knock at the door, not the front door though, the fairy door. She put the book on the armchair and headed to the door.

When Poppy opened the door, she saw little Amelia stood holding a basket of bread, flowers, cheese, juice, and apples.

'Hi, Poppy! Mummy sent me to give you these as a little welcome from the whole village!'

'Really? Wow, thank you! Would you like to come in and have tea with me?'

'Yes, please, Poppy!' Grinned Amelia before handing over the basket and entering the house.

'Wow, it's very nice in here, Poppy!'

'Thank you, Amelia. Here you go. Sit down. Would you like some juice?'

'Yes, please.'

Poppy was shaking as she took the basket from Amelia. She had never had a friend around for tea before. *What should she do?* She took out the juice from the basket and poured it into the glasses, trying to keep a steady hand. The juice was completely clear, and when Poppy sipped it, it was bland.

'What kind of juice is it?' asked Amelia

'I'm not sure. It just looks like water to me, Amelia!'

'No, you have to make it into juice by saying what it is!'

'Um, okay, pineapple juice?' and sure enough, the clear liquid turned an orange colour and tasted like pineapples when she sipped it. Every sip reminded her of her grandma and being back at home with her, but she couldn't cry or be sad now. She had a guest. She swallowed her tears and carried on, sipping her drink.

'See, but I don't like pineapple juice so much. Mine's apple juice,' said Amelia, and the liquid in the glass she was holding turned into the golden-colour apple juice and smelt like it too to Poppy.

'Wow, I didn't know you could do that. Do you want some cheese and bread, Amelia?'

As they ate and chatted all night, Poppy realised how young she really was although she was living alone and had to look after herself. But being with Amelia made her realise that she was only fourteen, just a couple of years older than the girl she was making tea for. She realised that she was still young enough to play with dolls, have teddy bear pick nicks, and was still young enough to go to school.

'Do you go to school, Amelia?'

'Next summer I start!' she announced proudly.

'So when is your birthday?'

'Next Saturday. I'm having a little party at my house. You can come if you like, Poppy. My friends are all a bit older than me because I'm the youngest fairy in Dreamland, but I like that. Everyone looks after me!' She grinned.

'Aw, you're very cute, Amelia. Am I your friend?'

'You're my best friend, Poppy. None of my other friends have let me have tea with them without their mummy being there. Where's your mummy, Poppy? My mummy talks about her a lot!'

Best friend? I haven't ever been called a friend before!

'My mummy, my mummy, um.' Tears began to well up inside Poppy, and she felt a huge lump in her throat that refused to go away. She swallowed it and blinked away the tears as she saw Amelia was waiting for an answer.

'"My mummy is in a very special place now. She was poor so she had to go away. She lives up in the sky, she plays in the clouds, she has some friends up there, and her mummy and daddy too live up there.' Poppy liked it like that. She felt happier if she said that her mummy and grandfather and grandmother were playing in the clouds, having fun in the sky.

'Wow, you're very grown up, Poppy. Am I your best friend?'

'Yes, Amelia, you are. You're the nicest, fair person I know! But it's getting late. Shall we take you back home to your mummy?'

Amelia looked sad to leave but agreed to go if she could come back and play tomorrow, so Poppy walked her home, and after having a little talk with Yasmina, she returned home.

Chapter Nine

Adjusting Life

Poppy had gotten used to life in Dreamland. She had made friends, her little house was perfect, and she made money from the beautiful clothes she made for the fairies, who paid highly for them. Although she loved life, talking to Yasmina, playing with Amelia, her best friend, making dresses, she missed her grandma and her house at the end of the forest, and she missed her dreams about the fairy prince. She had hardly seen him since she arrived, and he never came to her in her dreams anymore.

Chapter Ten

A New Poppy. A New Friend?

Poppy stared at herself in the mirror. She tugged at her long, limp hair. She frowned at the way it just laid around her head and didn't make her look attractive at all. Without a second thought, she grabbed the money she had from the dresses she had made for various fairies in the village and put them in her pocket and headed out of the door.

As she approached the hair salon, she saw inside two girls. They seemed to be laughing and joking with each other. Poppy was nervous to go in and stood still outside the window for a while, watching as one of the girls stood a little far back from the other, and Poppy watched as she pounced on the other's back. Poppy gasped and thought she should run in to stop them from fighting over whatever had happened. She ran to the door and burst in.

'Stop it at once, you two!' she cried, not even looking at them properly. 'You don't need to fight! I'm sure whatever has upset you is something you can talk about rather than use violence.'

The two girls sat on the floor and stared up at the little human girl that had just ran into their salon, for a few moments. Poppy and the girls stared at each other, all not sure what to say next.

Suddenly, the two girls burst into fits of laughter. They clapped their hands together, they rolled around on the floor, and at one point, they were silent, yet still laughing and clapping their hands like the seals Poppy once saw at the zoo with her grandmother.

'We aren't fighting! I was trying to give May a piggy back! But she is so fat I fell over,' said one of the two, through breaths of laughter.

'That's not very nice! To call your friend fat,' said Poppy, still not entirely sure what was happening here. She didn't know much about being friends, but she was sure this wasn't how to treat them.

'Don't worry. We were just having a bit of banter. April and I are best friends. We would never fight, and we both know we don't mean the horrible stuff we say about each other,' said the other, getting herself up from the floor and dusting the bits of hair off her clothes that hadn't been swept up yet.

'Wow, you must be really good friends to not get annoyed,' said Poppy in admiration.

'We are! Anyway, I'm May, and this is April! What can we do for you?' asked the other, standing up now.

Poppy looked at the fairies stood before her. April had shoulder-length glossy, curly dark purple hair with big green eyes and a friendly expression. She wore skintight jeans and a T-shirt that said 'I'm raw some!' with a picture of a dinosaur on the front. She looked very pretty and had lots of make-up on, making her look a lot older than Poppy thought she was. May, however, looked quite different. She had a short bob around her neck in brown colour that had a hint of red, the kind of red you would see on a strawberry, not the red that was orange, like flames around her head, the same hair Poppy's cousin William had.

May wore a plain black vest-type top and some blue floral shorts. Her legs were toned, and she wore black sandals around her blue—and yellow-painted toenails. She had a more natural face, without much make-up. She had a kind smile and warmness in her eyes. Both of them had a beautiful pair of silvery wings, the kind of wings Poppy longed to have. They were as shiny as glass but were as thin as paper and looked as light as a feather.

Poppy stuttered, 'Um, I wanted my hair.'

May took a sideways glance at April. 'You want what?'

Poppy suddenly realised what she had said and felt her cheeks turn red. 'Sorry, I mean, I want this sorting,' she said, pulling at her hair that hung around her head.

'Ah, yes. Well, sit here, and I'll see what I can do,' said April, shuffling Poppy into a big seat in front of a sink and mirror.

'Oh, not like I've done loads today, is it?' said May in a sort of sarcasm.

'What? Yes, you have, May!'

'No, I haven't! You did Mrs Dodd's and Julie's.'

'And you did Rosie's.'

They continued to bicker for a while until they were abruptly stopped by Poppy's frustration getting the better of her.

She stood up and stamped her foot. 'Look. Is anyone going to do my hair or are you going to stand there and argue all day? Just please, sort this mess out.'

She sat back down, and not another word was said about who does what. They did what they were supposed to.

Poppy stared at herself in the mirror for the second time that day.

This time, she grinned at her reflection. Most of the length was kept, but now her hair was layered and looked fuller. They had dyed it a lighter blonde and made it look healthy.

Although it was a small change, she felt like a new person. Poppy had spent most of the day with the girls. They laughed and joked and had a really good time.

Poppy knew the girls she had made friends with were true friends because they were so down to earth. They didn't care what people said or thought about them; they were just themselves. But they knew of the village gossip. That day, Poppy learnt that the man that owned the sweet stall was in love with the woman who owned the vegetable stall. April told her how she had a little ongoing conflict with Jacob, one of the boys in the village; they were boyfriend and girlfriend for nearly a year before it all ended badly. She also learnt that both April and May were in love with the same person, the baker's son, Sebastian, and that they often bickered with each other over him.

'You kissed him when you only went in for a scone the other day, April. How can you say you don't like him?'

'I know. I never said I didn't. I just don't want to do anything because I know you will be upset,' said April, trying to sound like a good friend.

'No, I won't. I don't like him. I like someone else,' said May in defence, suddenly clasping her hands over her mouth in shock at what she spat back at her sister.

'Oh my gosh! Who?' said April, now in shock.

'Well, you know that birthday party we went to a few weeks ago? I kissed Jacob,' said May, almost blushing. She flinched almost as if she was scared of what April's reaction would be.

'What?' whispered April, looking hurt.

May didn't say anything and just looked back at her sister with a 'don't hurt me' expression in her eyes.

'I can't believe you,' shouted April, before storming out of the shop.

Both Poppy and May watched through the window as she disappeared into the bakery door.

'I'm such a bad person,' cried May.

Poppy hated seeing her new friends fight, especially over a boy; when this happened, she grew a particular dislike for boys for making such good friends argue. But the news that shocked Poppy the most was that there was a rumour that the prince was to marry a flower fairy because the queen wanted to retire. Poppy's heart sank when she heard this, but she was determined to convince herself this wasn't true and was only gossip—gossip that wasn't true.

Chapter Eleven

One's Good News Is Another's Bad

One morning, Poppy was finishing the beautiful princess-styled dress she was making for Amelia for her birthday; it was a beautiful lilac dress, covered in little sparkles and flowers with a matching cardigan. Just as she was finishing the sparkles, she heard a knock at the door. She placed down the dress on her desk and shut the door. She was expecting Amelia, so she made sure she couldn't go in the same room where the dress was, but when she opened the door, there stood the fairy prince in all his handsomeness. His eyes were happy, and he smiled broadly at the sight of Poppy in her baggy trousers and T-shirt; her hair was tied up in a bun. She didn't look very attractive, but she sensed the prince didn't care. He just gazed at her.

'Have you lightened your hair, Poppy? It looks very nice!' was the first thing he said once Poppy had opened the door.

Poppy's face lifted. She smiled at the fact that the prince had noticed her hair and how she had changed. She also loved the fact he liked it.

'Hello, sir. I, um, I, come in!' Poppy couldn't think straight. He was so handsome for such a young boy. He was fifteen, only a year older than Poppy, but he had some manliness about him.

'Ha ha! Call me Alex, please, Poppy,' he chuckled as he entered her home.

The prince and Poppy stood in an awkward silence for a while, just both looking at each other, speechless. Poppy wished so much to be able to read the prince's mind to know what he was thinking about her.

'What can I do for you, Alex?' Poppy said, averting her eyes from his as she tried not to fall over or say anything stupid.

'I'd like you to make me a dress,' said the prince, suddenly coming out of his daze.

'Um, you want a dress?' That's when it hit Poppy hard as though a ton of bricks had been thrown on her head and a fist in her stomach. The rumours were all true. She felt sick with dizziness; the prince really was going to get married.

'Not for me, silly!' he smiled a warm smile.

'Oh, ha ha, sorry, whom for? What would you like it like?' she stammered. She felt the colour burning in her cheeks. She felt so stupid.

'A wedding dress,' he replied, a tone of false happiness in his voice.

'A what?'

The words echoed inside her. She felt like crying. Poppy was sure she was in love with him. *Who was he marrying?* So many more questions! She wanted to ask them all, right here, right now, but she couldn't. She didn't want him to know she cared.

'Don't tell anyone, but my mother wants to retire next year, and for her to do that, I must marry, but not just anyone. I have to marry a fairy, a well-behaved, do-good fairy. So I am meeting my bride tomorrow. She is from another fairy world. She is a flower fairy, and she will become the fairy princess,' he spoke, each word violently stabbing into Poppy as he spoke them. She was determined not to let her pain show, so she stammered.

'You've never met the person you will be with for the rest of your life? Don't you want to marry the person you love?'

His face seemed to look less happy as she spoke.

'It's too late for that. My mother wants to retire. She said her time on the throne is over now, and she wants to be a grandmother soon and enjoy the rest of her life. I'll never find the person I love. I just have to tell myself I love Sophia, my fiancée, and carry on,' he said quietly, almost in a whisper.

'But you're only fifteen! You're so young!'

'You're never too young to fall in love.' He handed Poppy a note and left her house.

Tears filled up in her eyes. She sat on the floor and cried until she felt she could cry no more. She was heartbroken. She had lost everyone, and now she had lost the prince. He was somebody else's. She had always dreamed of her wedding, her day, her love, her family, and now she was certain she could never have it. She knew she was still young, but none of the other fairies in the land matched up to the prince. Poppy's greatest fear was being alone, and now it was coming true.

She stood up and looked in the mirror: her hair was a mess, she wasn't dressed very nice, and her eyes were all puffy and red from crying. No wonder the prince didn't want to marry her. As she turned into her sewing room, she caught sight of Amelia's dress. She noticed how small it was and how it looked specially for a young little girl. She suddenly realised that she was also just a little girl and she shouldn't be so worried about whom she was to marry; that would happen in years to come. She should be happy for the prince and let him marry whoever he wanted. She had so many years to marry yet.

She set to work, making herself lots of beautiful cotton dresses, pink ones, yellow ones, blue ones, and white ones. From now on, she wasn't going to be scruffy and unpresentable; she was going to look pretty and nice. She put on one of the blue dresses and combed through her glossy blonde hair and tied it in a blue ribbon.

She remembered the note the prince had left her that she had dropped on the floor and picked it up. It was an invitation.

Miss Poppy Parish

Is invited by request of his royal highness Alexander of Dreamland to the Palace for a dress fitting with Miss Sophia Petal, future queen of Dreamland.

This information is strictly confidential.

Not to be shared with any other person.

Poppy felt tears welling up again; she felt a lump in her throat, and she felt the fist in her stomach again. But she said out loud, 'Stop it, Poppy. Grow up a bit. Be mature.' She swallowed hard to stop herself from crying. No longer did she feel a friend to the prince but one of his servants.

Chapter Twelve

Friend or Foe

The next morning, Poppy woke up and dressed in her new pink dress, combed her hair, and set off to the castle. She felt happy and very pretty in her new dress, and she skipped down the long lane towards the castle, humming a tune to herself. She passed the bakers and took a long deep breath in, inhaling the beautiful smell of bread, the same she did every day she passed it. She passed the hairdressers and waved to April and May, the hairdressing twins. They were the best friends and sisters, they were always laughing and smiling, and Poppy had grown to like them very much. Poppy passed the school and saw Amelia and her friends playing in the playground. She passed the florist and waved to Yasmina, who was making bouquets in the sun. She passed the vegetable store and the sweet stall and carried on skipping down the cobbled path; Right up to the castle gates, she spoke up to the guard, 'Hello, I'm Poppy, here to see the prince.'

He was a bit old; his face was grey and looked tired but brightened up when he saw Poppy.

'Hello there, okay, go straight in.' He smiled before opening the gates for her.

Poppy wandered through the palace gardens; they were beautiful, and there was every kind of flower growing in the flowerbeds. Poppy wanted to stop and gaze in awe of them all but knew she must go inside. She knocked on the big wooden doors, and they opened from the inside as she stepped into the wonderful marble floor. She looked around—the huge spiral staircase leading upwards, doors leading off to different rooms, people were rushing about here and there, flying up and down the stairs, in and out of doors, and somewhere, in the distance, a violin and a harp were playing a wonderful tune.

Suddenly, Poppy's skin crawled.

'You're so stupid, Rike! She's here now,' said a voice in the distance. It was that voice! From the forest, from the house. It was getting closer.

When they did appear, Poppy let out a little yelp; she was greeted by two very grotesque figures standing before her. They smiled with their yellow, crooked teeth that looked like needles in their mouths. One was tall and thin with a crooked, bony figure, and the other was nearly half the size of the other and very, very fat.

'Hello, your highness,' the tall one hissed like a snake, his bloodshot eyes staring into hers.

'Get back,' Poppy cried in terror. 'Who are you? I keep hearing your voice.'

Hearing Poppy's shouts, the fat one screamed and jumped into the other's arms, but as he was so large, he and his skinny friend collapsed on the floor in a heap.

'Stupid! What did you do that for?' said the skinny one, hitting his friend over the head hard.

'Rike! Pleased to meet you!' said the fat one. He had some short, greasy hair on top of his rounded head, and his yellow teeth emitted a horrible smell into the air. He held out a dirty hand and raised his black, bushy eyebrows.

'We're goblins, your highness,' said the skinny one, which seemed to be called Moss. He hissed a lot, and with his skinny, bendy figure, he reminded Poppy of a snake.

He had a greasy, tatty brown mop of hair that covered his eyes. He gave his head a shake to move it and revealed a spot-covered face and a wart on his fat nose, his ears stuck out, and his chin was long and pointed.

'We were sent to lead you to Dreamland,' said Rike.

'It was you two I heard running through the house. And you who got rid of the trees hiding the house?'

'You got that right! Although somehow Rike is the one with the magic in our family and can't use it at all!' Laughed Moss, ignoring Rike's hurt expression.

Poppy burst into laughter.

'Stop laughing at us! It's not very nice. You don't even know us very well. My mother would always say never judge a book by its cover,' whined Rike, biting his already short and dirt-filled nails.

'I'm laughing because goblins are stereotyped as very, very mean and very, very clever. It says so in my fairytales, and you seem to be extremely stupid, and I'm sure you can be nice!'

As Poppy regained herself, the fairy queen approached her. Poppy stared at her beauty, questioning whether that much of it was really possible.

'Hello, Poppy, you're here to see Alexander and Sophia. Am I right?'

'Yes, I'm making Sophia's wedding dress. What is Alexander's bride like?'

'Well,' the queen hesitated.

'She is very pretty,' she said at last.

'She's scary,' cried Rike.

'Shh! She's the future queen, stupid,' cried Moss, hitting his friend's head again.

Just as Poppy was about to question the queen's hesitation and Rike's comment, the prince entered the room with another fairy. She was very thin, and she had yellowy/green eyes that reminded Poppy of her next-door neighbour's cat Tabby's eyes. She was wearing a knee-length black dress that had a small slit up the right leg, and she looked very sophisticated with deep red lipstick and a lily clipped into her long, straight, black hair. Her wings didn't look clear and sleek like all the other fairies; they almost looked like feathers, or scales. Poppy soon discovered that they looked like petals, hence she was a flower fairy, but she never knew that you could get petals in such a dark blue/black colour, and Poppy had always imagined flower fairies in pink and green petal dresses with headbands and little barefeet, not in a sophisticated black dress and pointed heels like Sophia's. Everything was so backwards to the fairytales she knew. Sophia looked down her nose at Poppy who looked extremely young in her cotton dress and headband.

Poppy curtseied to the prince and Sophia, paying attention to tucking her foot behind her ankle and bending her knees to dip and curtsey, and as she rose, the prince spoke, 'Please, Poppy, don't curtsey. There is no need,' he chuckled.

Sophia looked at the prince with a look of disappointment, which then changed to distaste when she looked at Poppy. She sensed something between the two that she didn't like.

Both Sophia and Poppy looked shocked at his words, but before anyone could say anything, Poppy was pointing at Sophia's ankle and saying, 'If you don't mind me asking, miss, what is that?' Everyone followed the direction her finger was pointing and saw she was pointing at a chain of leaves in the skin of Sophia's bare ankle.

'It's a birthmark. It shows I am a flower fairy,' said Sophia, half in shock that Poppy had just asked the question.

'It's very beautiful! I have one of my own,' said Poppy, trying to be as friendly as she could towards the fairy, pulling down her collar. She revealed a dark brown splodge just below her neck, showing it off proudly

'THAT'S DISGUSTING!' cried Sophia. 'What kind of fairy are you?'

Poppy quickly put her dress back into place, covering up what she was told made her special and different from everyone else. She thought it was a good thing, maybe in the real world, but in Dreamland, certainly not.

'Um I'm not. I'm a human,' whispered Poppy, staring at the polished tiles on the floor.

Sophia giggled and said, 'Ah, so you're the maid making my dress. I did wonder who you were. Anyway, I don't want it too big, like a meringue.—'

'Maid? No, I'm a friend!' stammered Poppy, shocked that she was called a maid by a stuck-up girl she hardly knew. Already she was beginning to dislike this girl; she already didn't like because she was marrying the prince.

'Oh, your dress gave me the impression. Sorry!' Laughed Sophia.

Poppy shuffled, so she was slightly behind the queen's wings and crossed her arms. She was so embarrassed. She wanted to tear it off there and then and run home in tears, but she had to show she wasn't fazed by this new, snobby fairy.

After the rather rude remark from Sophia, the three fairies and Poppy stood in an awkward silence until Sophia spoke up, clutching the prince's hand as she did so.

'So, where are these dress ideas? I trust they are not like your own, so plain and simple and girlie.'

Poppy was glaring at the two fairies' interlocked fingers. She noticed Sophia's long slim fingers, hardly fitting in the gaps of the prince's, and her long, black painted nails. She was wearing a big sparkly ring on her wedding finger. It enchanted Poppy with its shine. She stood for some seconds, staring deep into the stone on her finger. Sensing this, Sophia pulled her hand away from the prince's and started to fiddle with her engagement ring.

'I, um, they, here you go, I think this one will be nice and fitting for your slim figure, and maybe some flowers down this side but not too overcrowd.'

'No, no,' cut in Sophia.

'I don't want one of your ideas. I want my own. I have it already planned. Here you go.' She handed Poppy a piece of paper with a sketch of the wedding dress she wanted. It was a long, rather big one, with a huge trail and lots of ruffles down the skirt.

'Okay, I'll go home and work on it now,' said Poppy quickly, wanting to get out of there as soon as possible because anger was bubbling inside her, and she was about to burst into tears.

She left through the gates, managing a smile for the guard at the gates, but behind the smile, her heart was breaking and tears were about to come, pouring out of her glossy blue eyes. She ran past the sweet stall in tears, she passed the vegetable stand, she didn't stop to wave at Yasmina, she didn't smile at April and May, she didn't even smell the bread when she ran past, she just ran into the door leading into her house, she dropped the picture of the wedding dress, she tore off her own dress, she climbed into the bed in her vest and pants, and she cried for a while and then lay silent in thought. *How could she have been so stupid?* She still loved the prince, but at the same time, she felt silly. She was so young. How did she know she was in love, but then she remembered the prince's words 'You're never too young to fall in love.' She didn't exactly know what love was, she didn't think the prince did either, but she was pretty sure this was something close. She was so angry with herself for letting Sophia talk to her the way she did. She was so angry with the prince for letting Sophia talk to her the way she did. Why did the prince want her to go to Dreamland so bad if she didn't even matter to him? Why didn't she matter to him? She lay in thought until finally she fell into a deep sleep.

In her dreams, she saw the fairy prince. He came to her, holding a log-stemmed pink flower in his hand.

Why was he visiting Poppy again? He hadn't been in her dreams since she came to Dreamland, and she couldn't understand why he was here now, just standing and holding a flower in his hand.

He was beginning to disappear, but he whispered the words 'Sorry' just before he was gone.

Chapter Thirteen

The Confession, the Complication

The next morning, when Poppy woke up, her eyes were stinging from all the crying, and she realised she was only in her vest and pants; she looked over at her dressing table mirror and saw her eyes were all red and puffy, and her cheeks were red. As she moved her head to put it back on her pillow, she realised the draw was open slightly; she didn't keep anything in the drawer and didn't remember opening it to put something in it. She stepped out of bed and went over to the dressing table. As she approached the drawer, she saw something pink in the back. She pulled open the draw further, and there, without a doubt, was the flower the prince was holding in her dream. As she reached in, she heard a loud knock at her door. She ran into the middle door and soon realised she didn't have anything on. She pulled on her nightie and opened the door.

Stood there, she saw the prince and Sophia. Today she was wearing some very high heels and a long, flowery, white summery dress. Her nails were painted a light pink, and she was wearing the usual heavy load of make-up, her hair was tied in a bun, and she looked about twenty, not fifteen, the age she really was. Poppy felt like running back into her bed and hiding, but she had to show she was strong, but she couldn't in her little pink nightie and puffy eyes.

'Oh, hi, sorry, I was just in bed. Please sit down and have a drink. I'll be done in a minute,' she said, leaving them at the door as she raced into her bedroom to get changed.

Poppy searched through her wardrobe. Everything looked so young and girlie compared to Sophia's outfits, and she rummaged through everything until she came to a dress she had packed in a hurry the day she left her house. It was small but was plain and navy blue. She squeezed into it and put on her flat, white dolly shoes, looking in the mirror; her dress hugged her figure and made her look nearly as sophisticated as Sophia. She combed her hair and ruffled it so it fell lightly around her shoulders. Poppy looked around her bedroom and put on a little bit of make-up, the one she kept for parties, but it would have to do for now.

'Sorry, what can I do for you both?'

The prince looked away from his glass of what looked like pineapple juice and his jaw dropped at the sight of Poppy.

She looked taller and older in the navy blue dress, her legs looked shapely, the make-up she wore and the way she let her hair fall outlined the perfect shape of her face, the eye make-up she had on made her blue eyes sparkle even more, and her lips were pink and looked like they were slightly pouted with the glossy lip shimmer she had put on.

'Um, you look,' before he could even finish, Sophia turned from looking at the photos of Poppy and her mother the day Poppy was born and cut in, 'like you're about to go to a party. You're a bit overdressed, aren't you, Poppy?' she said, looking her up and down.

'No, actually, I just thought I'd make an effort for such good guests.' She smiled, hiding the fact she wanted to pounce on Sophia and tear her hair out.

'Amazing,' said the prince in a breath.

Poppy's heart skipped a beat as she heard the words come from the prince's mouth.

'Anyway, we're here because I want to see my dress,' said Sophia, turning from the pictures and to the prince.

'Oh, I haven't even started it yet, Sophia,' said Poppy, glancing at the piece of paper she had thrown on the floor the night before.

'Excuse me?' said Sophia, with a slight smile on her face, almost as if she was happy it wasn't done.

'She hasn't started it yet. I told you she might need time, Sophia,' said the prince.

'Be quiet, Alex. You don't know how easy it is to make a dress. I could have done it by now, have it done by tomorrow morning. Come on, Alex,' she said before storming off.

The prince looked torn; he wanted to stay with Poppy whose eyes were welling up. He wanted to make her feel happy again. She was too beautiful to crumple her face and let her eyes smear her make-up she had beautifully painted on. He wanted to hug her; he understood how Sophia was being so cruel to her because she knew how Poppy loved the prince. He could read Poppy's mind, and he knew anger was boiling inside her and knew she was angry with him for letting Sophia talking to her the way she did, but he also knew that Sophia was a scary fairy and she was very controlling, so he turned to leave, but as he did, he said, 'Did you find my flower?'

'Yes I did. Why, Alex?'

'I felt bad about what Sophia said to you. I thought I'd let you know. I couldn't stay for long or do too much because Sophia would know I was in your dream, so I just gave you the flower and had to leave.'

'Thank you, but I wasn't asking why you left the flower. I want to know why you're marrying her.'

'You know why, Poppy, I have to. I love her.'

You're just a child! How can you say that?

'No, you don't. Don't lie to yourself, Alex. You're only doing it because you need to become a king. Can't you see she doesn't love you? She just wants to be a queen. You're just a child. You don't love her!'

'Don't call me a child! I'm older than you. You don't know how I feel. You can't tell me that. Sophia and I love each other.'

'Get out,' said Poppy through gritted teeth, staring at the floor. She hated him so much; he just let Sophia talk to her like she was a piece of dirt on the floor. She hated Sophia too. She didn't even know what Poppy had done to annoy her, but she wasn't going to let it happen.

Poppy went to where the drawing of the wedding dress was and picked it up. Looking at it, she didn't even like the style of it, or maybe she did, but she didn't want to because Sophia had drawn it.

She shoved it in her pocket and ran out of her house, slamming the door behind her. The prince was half way up the cobbled path by now, and it looked like Sophia was already at the castle.

Poppy walked very quickly with her eyes glaring at the palace. She didn't move them, and she just fixed her eyes on the gates and didn't look away. She forgot to smell the bread and look through the hairdresser's window, and she didn't even reply to Yasmina when she shouted hello.

The prince was just in front of her, but she stormed past him without moving her eyes from the palace. She got to the gates and pushed them open by herself, stunning the guard who was only just walking over to open them for her. Poppy was in such a rage she didn't realise the prince was now running after her. She stepped in the flowerbeds, crushing the flowers with her feet. She didn't follow the path round to the door, and she stormed across the wet grass, getting madder and madder.

She passed Rike and Moss practicing magic on a tree—turning into a pig and then something else—and didn't bother to ask what they were doing.

As Poppy approached the front doors, she knocked on them hard. They opened from the inside and just coming down the stairs was Sophia.

'Sophia!' Poppy cried, her voice echoing the room.

'What do you want? Do you have permission to come here?' said Sophia, not moving from the step she was on.

'Don't worry, I'll be going soon. I wouldn't want to stand in your presence for too long, and I dread the day you become a queen. I'm tired of the way you treat me. I was once the prince's friend, but you have turned me to his servant. So if you are so amazing, and as you said, you could have made it by now, you can make your own wedding dress,' she said, crumpling up the paper and throwing it at her.

'Snookie? Are you seriously going to let her do this to me?' Sophia addressed the prince who was now standing behind Poppy.

'Snookie?' Laughed Poppy before noticing the prince stepping forward.

'Yes,' he replied to Sophia.

Both Poppy and Sophia looked shocked. Sophia grabbed hold of the bannister as if she was about to fall.

'Sorry, I thought you just said yes that you were going to let this little non fairy talk to your love like this.' Sophia laughed.

'No, I'd never let that happen,' replied the prince.

Poppy sank her head at the words and got ready for the prince to shout. She hated him even more now. She knew the prince didn't really love Sophia; he was just doing it for his mother. She couldn't believe he was sticking up for her and not Poppy whom he had begged to come to Dreamland.

By now, the queen had heard the commotion and peered through the door and watched as the three stood; none of them was entirely sure what was going on.

'You're right, Sophia. I would never let anyone, fairy or not, talk to the one I love like she did to you, but you're not the one I love, Sophia. I've been fooling myself these past few days. I've been fooling you, Sophia, and I've been fooling my mother, and the only person I couldn't fool was Poppy. I'm sorry, Sophia, but I can't marry someone who puts others down because of the way they look, and I can't marry you, Sophia,' the prince spoke out, confidently. Poppy wanted to jump around laughing, but she controlled herself and stayed quiet as she saw Sophia's eyes began to cry.

The prince turned to Poppy.

'Poppy, you're absolutely beautiful. You don't need to dress like someone you're not because you think I will love you more.'

'What?' Sophia and Poppy both said in unison.

'You made me realise, Poppy. I love you. I always have, and I love you whether you're in little girlie dresses or not. I love you when you look grown up. I love you in your scruffy jeans and jumper. You're beautiful, and I love you any way you look. Please don't change it.'

'Well, I love you!' cried Poppy, throwing her arms around his neck.

The prince and Poppy hugged and looked into each other's eyes lovingly. This was the first time they had ever felt the way they did, but it was such a short moment. It was interrupted by the harsh, cold, slow laughing of Sophia. But Poppy didn't care. She was in love; she was happy, and nothing could burst her bubble until Sophia's words like tiny daggers burst it cruelly.

'Ha ha! Don't be so stupidly silly,' she spat down at them. 'You're too young to be in love, little girl,' said Sophia, smugly.

'And anyway, Alex, you can't marry her or even love her. If you want to make your silly mother dear happy and become a king, you have to marry me. You can't marry a little girl,' she continued, obviously pleased with herself.

'You're never too young to be in love.'

The words came from further down the hallway. Everyone's head turned towards the familiar voice. They had been so focused on Sophia, and no one had realised the fairy queen standing beside them, listening to the whole conversation.

'Sophia, I am not prepared to allow my son to marry such a cold-hearted, power-hungry girl, and why you keep calling Poppy a little girl? She may be young, but she is so much more mature than you. She is kind and cares for others, whereas you, you only care about yourself,' said the queen, calmly.

'Now, please, get your stuff and leave,' she finished.

'Don't be stupid. You know if he doesn't marry me, he can't become a king,' said Sophia, unfazed of the queen's harsh words.

'I know, but he can if he marries the fairy he truly loves.' Smiled the queen, looking towards Poppy and the prince who had his arm around the very perturbed and frightened-looking Poppy.

'Ha ha!' Laughed Sophia, slowly. There it was again. Poppy cringed when she heard it—the slow, saddening laugh of Sophia's snobby voice.

'You just said it yourself, your highness. Alex must marry the fairy he loves, and all I see before me is a silly little *human* girl,' Sophia smirked.

'Exactly,' replied the queen. 'That's why I wish for Poppy to become a fairy at a royal ceremony I hold, if the prince's and Poppy's love is true, she will have her own wings and magic. And it's, 'his highnesses to you.'

Poppy gasped at the thought of becoming a fairy and smiled broadly; the prince cheered and they. hugged, delighted again.

'NO,' screamed Sophia. 'I was meant to become a queen, me. Not her!'

As the queen opened her mouth to speak, Poppy stepped forward, and up a couple of steps, so she was the same height as Sophia, and calmly, she said, 'It takes courage, kindness, and love for people to become a queen, Sophia, and those three things are things you lack. I'm sorry, but as your beauty and sophisticatedness is high, your personality is very low.'

'Exactly, now, I demand you to leave,' said the prince.

Sophia's face scrunched up, and she began to wail. She looked ugly to the prince and even uglier to Poppy because she never looked pretty to Poppy, maybe on the outside but never on the inside. Sophia ran out of the castle and ran into the station, throwing the engagement ring at the prince as she did so.

The prince bent down and picked up the ring and balanced on one knee. He looked up at Poppy, taking her hand.

'Will you, Poppy Parish, become a fairy and my wife?' His eyes gazed into hers like he did in her dreams, his eyes burned into her mind lovingly, and he wanted to take her in his arms and never let anyone hurt her ever again, but he had to wait for an answer. It seemed he was waiting for hours for an answer, but really it wasn't even seconds before Poppy cried the words he was wishing and waiting for.

Chapter Fourteen

The Announcement

Poppy woke up and smiled broadly. The events of yesterday crept up on her, and she was so happy. She felt like flying. Soon she would be able to! She held out her hand in front of her and was mesmerized by the jewel's sparkle. She was enchanted just like the first time she saw the ring, but this time, it was on her finger, not Sophia's.

She got up, and in her nightie, she shuffled, half asleep into her study, seeing the dress she had made for Amelia. She suddenly remembered Amelia's birthday! She rushed into her bedroom and put on a lilac dress, a similar one to the one she had made for Amelia.

She pulled up her hair into a sophisticated bun and put on some make-up like she had done the previous day. She had to keep a good image if she was to become Alex's wife, let alone a princess.

As Poppy arrived at the florists, she could hear music and children's laughter. She saw Amelia sat at a table with a plastic tiara on; her friends were dressed as prince and princesses, too. Poppy entered excitedly and realised how much she wanted to join in; she realised how young she really was. She was going to get married at the young age of fourteen. To a prince! She wanted so badly for her friend Jade at school to be there so she could tell her about everything. She was constantly trying to better her friend, and she was the friend with the big house, the many pets, and the *parents*. But Poppy knew Jade would soon stop her boasting if she knew about this, but she couldn't do it. She was never to return, never to go to school again, never to see her friends. Before her trail of thoughts had chance to continue, Amelia's happy voice interrupted, 'Poppy! Yay! I'm so glad you're here!' She cried, running over and giving her a hug.

'Happy birthday, Amelia.' Smiled Poppy, handing over the dress she had made as Yasmina came over to welcome Poppy.

'Wow, it's beautiful! What do you say, Amelia?' Yasmina chuckled.

'Can I put it on, please?' begged Amelia.

'Not until you thank Poppy!'

'Oh, yes, sorry, thank you so much, Poppy,' said Amelia, excitedly, before running off to show her friends. As she did, Poppy noticed a small cloud like picture on Amelia's wrist.

'What's that mark on Amelia's wrist?' asked Poppy to Yasmina.

'Her birthmark. Every fairy has one. Hers is cloud, and mine shows that we are dream fairies,' she said, pulling off her shoe revealing a cloud printed on her foot near the start of her toes.

'Wow! That's incredible! My birthmark's disgusting. Does that mean I'm disgusting?' said Poppy, feeling young and silly, like a little girl asking her mother why the girls at school laugh at her.

'Let's see it then,' said Yasmina, sensing Poppy's insecurity.

'Sophia told me it was disgusting. I'm not too sure if I want this,' fidgeted Poppy.

'I'm sure Sophia is just trying to make you worried.' Winked Yasmina.

As Poppy agreed and pulled down her collar, Yasmina smiled and said, 'Ah, yes, I've seen one just like that before!' she said.

'Really? On who?'

'A very special woman, your mother, of course.'

'Oh yes, what does my birthmark show I am?'

'Individual.' Smiled Yasmina.

Poppy felt so young again and was soon reminded of what she must face today. Her stomach lurched as she said, 'Sorry, Yasmina, I have to leave to do something,' checking her watch and hiding her ring behind her back. No one knew about the engagement yet, until the announcement later on today.

'Oh, okay, well, thanks for stopping by!' She grinned. 'Oh, have you heard? We all have to be in the palace gardens in an hour. Apparently, there is an announcement. Everyone knows about Sophia, so I wonder what it is!' said Yasmina in thought.

Poppy smiled; she felt happy in a way that she was the only person who knew about the announcement and was part of it! She couldn't wait for her friends to find out. She said goodbye to them and left for the palace.

She skipped up the cobbled path, her heart pounding. The last time she walked towards these gates, she was going to talk to the future princess of Dreamland. Now she is the future princess, walking towards her future home, her future husband, her future life.

She was such a mess inside. Part of her wanted to jump for joy and scream and run and tell every fairy she came across her amazing news. But the other part of her wanted to go and crawl into her bed and cuddle up and hide from the world and its challenges. But the biggest part of her wanted, more than anything, to go back to the little house outside of the forest, back through the conservatory doors, and cuddle up with her grandmother on her big armchair. She wanted her mother to come through the door and kiss her head and read to her. She wanted that so much, if she could, right now, she would leave everything behind and go back to her old life.

Poppy stopped on the cobbled path; she turned her head and looked around her. She was nearly at the gate, but she wanted to run back, back to her old life, back to grandma, but she took a deep breath and told herself, 'This is my new life now. There's no going back.' She smiled and carried on walking, her head held high.

The guard let her in as usual; he was obviously clueless to the announcement, as well as everybody else in Dreamland.

As soon as Poppy was let into the castle, she saw the prince stood in the main hall in all his glory. The moment he saw her, he grinned like a silly child, and the part of Poppy that wanted to run back home evaporated. The prince, surprisingly, gently took Poppy by the waist, feeling her perfect curves under her silky dress, pulled her towards him, leant down to her level as he was a few inches taller than Poppy, the way they both liked it, and kissed her softly on the lips. They seemed to kiss for a matter of minutes to the maids and the other fairies that were in the palace watching joyfully from afar, but to Poppy and her future husband, it was so short-lived, and they wanted it to last forever.

Fireworks. All that Poppy could see was fireworks. She knew from that moment, from that kiss, that she truly loved the prince.

She opened her eyes to see his face, nearly touching hers, smiling at her, the same loving gaze he had when he came to her in her dreams.

'I've never kissed Sophia. I suppose I never wanted to. But you, I could kiss you all day if I could, Poppy. I love you,' said the prince, hugging her closely, taking in her sweet perfumery scent.

Poppy's heart skipped a beat again; she was still recovering from the shock of yesterday. She didn't know she could handle this. She was acting so cool, so calm, so collected, but inside, she was jumping about screaming, cheering, laughing. But she didn't know if she loved the prince. *How did she know what love was? Was it the fireworks, the way she could never stop thinking about the prince, the way they kissed, or the way she was lost for words around him?* She wasn't certain, but she was pretty sure that was exactly that.

'It's okay,' the prince continued. 'I know you feel the same way too, Poppy. I can see it in your mind.'

'I love you,' said Poppy, almost breathless. Her legs, brain, and stomach were like jelly; she could hardly stand, let alone speak.

The fairy queen entered the room and smiled at the prince and Poppy standing closely together, smiling, and well, just being in love. She knew this was the right thing to do.

'Sorry, to err, interrupt,' the queen hesitated, not wanting to ruin the moment. 'But, Poppy, we must get you ready for the announcement. You two look adorable together!' she chuckled, before heading upstairs.

'I'm so nervous!' Poppy whispered to the prince. 'What if they don't want me as princess?'

'Well, that won't matter, Poppy, because you're not becoming the princess. You're becoming the queen.' The prince smiled. 'And they are going to love you. You haven't got a bad bone in your body. I love you, and that's all that counts. Now go and get ready!' He kissed her cheek lightly before going to have a stroll in the gardens whilst Poppy followed where the queen went.

She had never been anywhere else in the palace other than the main hall in the entrance, so she took everything in, just like she had done with her home the first time she found it. She carried on up the red-carpeted stairs, holding on to the big wooden banister with her tiny hands; her nails she had painted a nice pearly pink colour to match the dress she would wear. She looked around the walls surrounding the staircase; there were pictures of late fairy kings and queens and princes and princesses. Most of the men were called Alexander; Poppy guessed that the name was passed down, generation to generation. From her countings, the prince she was about to marry was Alexander, the fifth. She was about to become prince Alexander, the fifth's wife. She smiled at the title before coming to a corridor leading to some rooms. One of the doors was open, so Poppy peered her head around the door, and inside was a large room with just a table and chairs. It looked like a large dining room; on the walls were different paintings by different artists, and there was a large black piano in the corner of the room. She suspected someone would play whilst they ate. One side of the room was completely made of glass and four very large shiny windows hid behind some thin, white curtains.

Poppy stepped into the room, on to the wooden floor and went over to the windows; she moved the curtain a little and had a look out of the window. Outside was a huge grand balcony, overlooking the palace gardens and Dreamland. Poppy saw the cobbled path, the florists, the hairdressers, the school, the bakery, and a very little house, which was her own. She looked at the forest around the house; it went on for miles. You couldn't see her grandmother's house. Poppy smiled at the magic she knew that was hiding Dreamland from the rest of the world just as she heard a lovely singing from the corridor. Being as curious as she was, Poppy left the room to find the voice she had heard.

Leaving the room, she saw a maid flying around here and there. And out of her mouth came the beautiful singing Poppy had heard. As the maid caught sight of Poppy, she stopped singing and flying and landed in front of her. She curtsied politely.

'Oh, no, please, miss, don't curtsey for me!' Laughed Poppy.

'Oh, okay.' Smiled the maid.

'What's your name?' questioned Poppy.

'My name, miss, is Lucy,' replied the maid.

'That's a beautiful name! I'm Poppy. Could you tell me where I am to get ready, Lucy?' she asked.

'Yes, just that room there,' said Lucy, pointing to a door on the left, opposite the dining room.

'Thank you, Lucy! I hope we can be friends,' said Poppy with a smile as Lucy flew off into a different room.

As Poppy entered the room, her mouth made a huge 'O' shape in shock. In the middle was a huge four-poster bed with a light pink netted curtain around it, much different to the little single bed she had at home. The floor was carpeted in a cream-coloured material, and there was a very large window behind big, heavy pink curtains on one side of the room. On another side were a grand dressing table and stool, a large wardrobe, and a shiny mirror. Poppy closed and locked the door and got out the dress she had made to wear for the announcement.

It was a light, pearly pink colour. It was long and trailed on the floor about two inches behind her, and there were a few layers with little sparkles around the top and long sleeves of the dress. She stepped into it and placed her feet in some small heeled, matching pink shoes. She put her hair in loose curlers whilst she sat down at her dressing table and put some powder on her nose. She put some pinky gloss on to her lips and put the powder on her cheeks so that she outlined her cheek bones and face shape. The eye make-up she put on made her eyes look bigger and shinier.

She took out the curlers from her hair, and it fell bouncily around her face in large waves. Just as she was spraying her favourite sweet rose perfume Yasmina had made for her from the roses from her shop, she heard a knock at the door.

The fairy prince spoke, 'Are you ready, Poppy? It's time.'

Poppy took a deep breath and opened the door.

This time, it was the prince's heart that skipped a beat; he couldn't believe his eyes when he saw the beauty that was his fiancée.

'How do I look?' asked Poppy, sensing the prince's amazement.

'Like a queen,' said the prince.

Poppy took the prince's arm, and they were led into the room opposite. Poppy wondered how they were going to announce the engagement to Dreamland in the dining room. Then she remembered. The balcony!

In the room, the fairy queen waited for them to enter and told Poppy to sit at the table and wait for her to be called through to the balcony. As the balcony doors were opened, the queen stepped through. Poppy caught sight of the thousands of fairies outside in the gardens. All she could say was 'wow' but even then she just whispered it to the prince before he followed the queen out into the balcony.

Even though the doors were shut behind them, she could see the prince's tall, muscly silhouette and the dainty one of the queens, surrounded by her wonderful blue gown she had worn for the occasion. Poppy could hear every word. She heard the crowd fall deadly silent as they stepped out and not even a cough was heard as the queen spoke, 'My dear people, I have invited you hear today to tell you some good news. Some wonderful news in fact. But it is not my news. It is my son's. I hope you will agree with me that this truly is an amazing news!'

The queen stepped back as the prince stood up to the front. He placed his hands on the hard stone of the balcony and spoke out to his people, 'Hello. Again, thank you for coming to hear my announcement. As you probably knew, the rumour got out that I was to marry. The rumour also got out that I was to marry a fairy named Sophia. I can now tell you that the rumour was true.'

Still, not even a breath could be heard from the thousands down below. They just stood, staring up in silence.

'But to become a great princess, to become a great queen, you must be kind, courteous, and courageous. You must be giving, thankful, and joyful. But to be my queen, you must be all of these but so much more. To be my queen, I must love you. And you must love me back. I'm sad to say that Sophia did not share this love with me, and without it, she could not be my queen. She could certainly not be yours. I was going to marry her, for my dear mother's sake, but there was someone who made me realise that Sophia and I did not have the love we needed to rule over Dreamland. That someone has made me realise that it is her I truly love and her I want to be my wife and the queen.'

Poppy's eyes filled up with the prince's speech. She knew with all her heart that the prince loved her like she loved him. And the moment she stepped out on to the balcony was the moment the whole of her world would change. Everybody would know of the love they shared, and Poppy would no longer be the little girl everyone knew her as. She would be the mature, the beautiful, the fairy, and the queen, Poppy.

'So now, I would like you to meet my future wife, your future queen,' the prince continued with delight.

Poppy stood up, shaking, and she walked over to the balcony doors, and as they opened, she took a deep breath and smiled at the people below her as she stepped forward on to the balcony.

They all stood in silence, still, but this time from pure shock at the little girl stood before them. All the fairies, apart from one! Amelia jumped up and down in excitement; amazingly, she shouted, 'That's my best friend, Poppy!' The whole crowd heard, and everybody cheered and jumped around in excitement.

A few tears slipped down Poppy's cheeks as she saw how happy Amelia was and how happy Dreamland was to welcome Poppy as their queen. Poppy waved to Amelia and Yasmina, and April and May, and all her other fairy friends. The prince took Poppy's hand, and as he did, and as they waved, they both whispered at exactly the same time, 'I love you.'

As they spoke the three words, hand in hand, Poppy started to feel a tingle all over her body; she let go of the prince's hand, and she began to glow. The crowd had noticed the strange glow around Poppy's body and all stood in silence now. They watched as Poppy began to hover; she was somehow up in the air. They saw the scared look all over Poppy, and they saw two golden wings grow from her back.

Suddenly, the glow around her stopped, and she floated back down to the balcony. She turned round to see the reflection of her in the balcony door; there she stood, in all her beauty, with golden wings attached to her back.

Poppy looked shocked, so did all the fairies watching her. The prince and the queen smiled as she began to laugh at her reflection. She began to giggle; she was so happy! She jumped up into the air and flew into the crowds, arms outstretched, and her hair flowing, wild and free. She flew around the tree tops with the birds and flew around the palace; everyone's head followed her journey. She flew back down and placed her feet on the ground. Right in front of Amelia! Without a word, she smiled and hugged her best friend. She then took her hand and pulled her into the air with her. Hand in hand, they flew above the crowd, laughing and smiling as they went. And one by one, each fairy flew up off the ground and joined them in the sky. Everyone flew around, laughing and cheering. Even the prince and the queen! The band from inside the castle played wonderful music and every fairy in Dreamland was up in the sky, flying around laughing.

Poppy wished her mother could see her. She wished her grandmother could see her, up in the clouds, with all her dearest friends, about to become a queen.

Chapter Fifteen

Back to the Real World

Poppy lay in bed; she stared up to the ceiling and imagined her wedding with the prince. She could see her walking up the isle to meet her prince. She designed her wedding gown in her head, and soon she became sleepy and shut her eyes.

She was quite surprised when she saw the prince staring back at her when she closed her eyes, and he didn't stare into her eyes like usual, but he did bring the warm, happy feeling to Poppy like he always did.

'Come outside,' said the prince before disappearing.

Poppy opened her eyes and saw her ceiling again. She sat up, pulled on one of her little cotton dresses, tied up her hair, and headed out of the door after putting on her shoes without a second thought.

She wasn't too sure where she was meant to go, but she went through the small forest separating her house from the cobbled path. She had never been through these trees when it was dark and found it hard to see.

Suddenly, she felt a big hand clasp around her arm. Poppy screamed as the hand dragged her down into the bushes. She struggled with the body holding her, causing them to roll down the tree-scattered hill. Poppy screamed and struggled with the body she couldn't see, which was refusing to let go of her. They now had both hands clinging to her arms, and as they stopped rolling and lay still, breathless from struggling, Poppy was now on top of this stranger. She kicked and wriggled as much as she could. She even flapped her wings, trying to fly away still screaming. The stranger pulled Poppy closer to him, his strength overpowering Poppy's small frame, and he pulled her into him, his body warming hers. They were nose to nose, and Poppy stopped struggling. She somehow felt safe now, happier, and warmer.

She felt his warm breath on her face and felt his muscles tense around her; the figure holding her seemed to be familiar and friendly. He lifted his head so his nose was now side to side to hers; he tilted his head, and his lips touched hers.

Poppy relaxed into his arms; she kissed him back, and his grip loosened on her arms, and she stretched them round his head, felt his soft hair between her fingers, and felt his hands run through her hair.

'Hello,' said the prince through the darkness.

'You scared me so much!' said Poppy, hitting him in the arm playfully.

'Stop it!' he cried, grabbing her hand and holding it.

Poppy remembered Sophia's skinny fingers, not fitting into the gaps between the princes, and she smiled when she realised hers fit perfectly.

She rolled over and lay next to him as they lay, hand in hand, catching their breath from the struggle they had.

'Alex, do you know what happened to my grandmother? I've been thinking about her a lot recently,' whispered Poppy.

'Yes, some fairies carried her up to heaven. She is with your mother and grandfather now.'

'What about my house?'

'I'm not sure. I suppose it's just empty now, waiting for someone to discover it.'

'Wow. The stuff I left in there the day I left in a hurry! I'd give anything to go back there now.'

The prince turned on his side and leant to her ear and whispered into it, 'What about a kiss?'

Poppy sat up with a start in the darkness.

'I can't. My grandmother said I must never go back.'

'Poppy, she said that because she didn't want you to be swapping alive. You won't if we just go now. You can get some stuff and never go back. You have to promise that, Poppy. You must never go back after that. I just want to make you happy.'

'I just want to know everything's okay,' she whispered, and she leant over and kissed the prince.

He leapt up, and Poppy let him lead her back up the hill they had fallen down and back into her house. When they got inside, Poppy went into her room and took a coat and a torch. The prince waited by the door that led to the real world. He put his hand on the doorknob and whispered, 'Ready?'

When Poppy had nodded, she found herself making the journey she used to when she didn't even know of the fairies. Now she was a fairy, leading a fairy prince over the little wooden bridge, up the steep bank, and through the trees as the silver moonlight poured over them.

Once they had gone through the branches, Poppy stood still on the spot she was in. She shone the torch on the ground on a patch of daisies, and tears welled up in her eyes as she remembered sitting here whilst her grandmother was in the garden. She looked over to the garden, and she saw her grandmother's cottage so close now. It was dark and looked unloved; the garden her grandmother once put so much love and effort into was now overgrown and tangled; the grass was long, and weeds had overtaken the once colourful flower bushes.

The prince took her hand and tugged her a little. She felt frozen in the spot she was standing in, and she was terrified of what she would find in the house. The prince tugged again, and she took a step forward and felt him pulling her through the severely overgrown grass and weeds. She felt a sharp pain in her leg as she realised they had gone past some nettles. Now everything felt real; nothing was backwards or confusing in the real world, but it was cruel and cold, a world full of death and loss and bad luck and hurt. A world she was glad she wasn't part of now.

'Turn your torch off, Poppy. What would the neighbours say? That they saw a light and then two fairies walking through a garden they thought was deserted?' The prince laughed.

Poppy turned off her torch just as they got to the door.

'Ah, how to get in?' said the prince.

Poppy took the handle and pushed hard, and the door swung open. 'I didn't lock it when I left, oops!' She laughed, now stepping into the house.

She felt along the dusty wall for the light switch. She clicked it on and blew the thick black dust from her hand. They stumbled over the pile of post that was left by the door. Poppy sifted through it, finding some birthday cards addressed to her. Putting these in her pocket, she found that the rest looked like bills and catalogues. Looking around the kitchen, it looked exactly the same as the day she left it, the few pots still left in the sink. As she felt her leg throb, she grabbed a towel off the side and went to the cupboard and took out the vinegar, dabbing it on the sore red lumps on her leg. She said, 'Everything's the same as I left it.' She swallowed hard, not sure if she was swallowing tears of pain or of sadness of this cold, dirty, empty house she once loved.

They moved into the hallway, and Poppy went into the living room. She looked at the armchair she used to curl up on with her grandma whilst watching Saturday night TV or reading wonderful books. She went over to the chest near the window and opened the drawer and took out a scrap book she had made with her grandmother one rainy afternoon. The prince stood over her shoulder, looking at the pictures and daisy chains she had stuck in as she flicked through the pages. She closed the drawer and the book and carried it with her as she took the bannister and slowly went up the stairs. The whole house seemed to creek and shudder scarily with each step she took. This house, she once loved, was now somewhere she wanted to leave and never return to. She stood before three doors: the bathroom, her grandmother's room, and her room.

She walked towards her own room and reached for the handle, but her hand dropped back to her side. She turned to the other door and slowly edged the door open, and the room was dark inside and felt empty and lonesome. She put her hand in through the darkness and watched it disappear. She shivered from the cold and glanced behind her, making sure the prince was close to her. She turned on the light and could see the shape of her grandmother's bed and window, and Poppy took a deep breath and stepped inside. She walked over to her grandmother's empty, neatly made bed, but it wasn't made by her grandmother. She always folded over the top of the duvet and put one pillow on top of the other, but the pillows were next to each other and the duvet not folded. Poppy remade her grandmother's bed, and as she finished, she felt her legs collapse underneath her. She fell to the floor and cried whilst the prince put his arm around her and tried to comfort her.

He hated seeing her cry and tried to make her feel better.

'She's okay now. She is happy, Poppy.'

Poppy sniffed and nodded her head as the prince took her hand, helped her stand up, and led her out of the room and into her own, closing the door behind them.

The prince sat down on Poppy's little pink bed, still not made from the day that she left. Poppy was always getting told off for not making it. She opened her wardrobe and searched inside for a bag. The only one she could find was her school bag. She poured out her pens, pencils books, and folders on to her bed beside the prince and put in her letters and scrap book.

The prince scanned a blue book Poppy had emptied from her bag and smiled at the words written on the page.

'You're very good at writing stories.' Smiled the prince.

'Really? They are just things I write down when I'm bored,' said Poppy whilst going through her clothes, most of them being too small for her now.

The prince came to a small verse, but instead of scanning through it, he read the four lines over and over again.

Love.

What is love?

Does it come to you in your dreams?

Do its eyes burn into your mind, and never stop?

Yes. That is love.

The prince read it out loud, and Poppy froze in her search. She turned to the prince who by now had finished and was smiling.

'What's this?' he questioned.

'You know perfectly well what it is, Alex,' said Poppy, blushing.

'No, I don't,' he smirked.

'When I was only young, before my grandmother, you know when you would come to me. You so loved, so kind, so warming, I truly felt I loved you,' said Poppy, wanting to hide her burning red cheeks.

'Really, you've loved me all this time?'

'I suppose. I thought it was impossible to love at that age. I always told my friend Jade she was stupid for telling her boyfriend she loved him at the age of thirteen, but then I fell in love with you. Stupid really.'

'Loving me is stupid?' said the prince, saddened.

'No, the fact I told her she was silly for saying what I do to you. You know I love you, don't you? And anyway, I'm almost fifteen, so I'm not as silly.'

The prince hugged her and helped her pack a few treasures in her bag, and Poppy said her very final goodbye to the house and left. Again!

Chapter Sixteen

A Dream Came True

Poppy was so happy with her wings; every so often, she would lift off the ground and fly around for a bit.

When Poppy had returned from spending the day at the palace, she kicked off her shoes and sunk into her armchair. She reminisced the night she became a fairy and softly fell asleep, dreaming of the night and how it would be different if her mother was there.

Suddenly, in her sleep, Poppy could see a bright light. It was a little in the distance, but she could make out a tall woman silhouette. It was walking towards her. Poppy was terrified, but at the same time, she wanted to know who this woman was walking towards her. She heard the slow tap of the woman's heels as she took each step. She heard them echo in her mind. She heard them get louder as she got closer. Soon enough, she could see the woman's long, white flowing skirt and black top. She could see her hair combed neatly around her face. That was the only problem. Poppy couldn't see the woman's face; it was still shadowed by the light from behind her.

Soon enough, the woman became clear to Poppy. It was her mother.

'Hello, Poppy,' the woman spoke out, warmly, with tears in her eyes.

Poppy began to cry. She couldn't believe it. She had dreams about her mother before, but she knew this really was her mother. She knew she was real.

'Please don't cry,' her mother begged. 'I had to come and see you. Now you're a fairy. You can summon anyone to your dreams. As you were thinking about me, I heard your thoughts and came to you.'

'I don't understand?' whimpered Poppy.

'You're a dream fairy now, Poppy. Look!' She pulled Poppy's collar down and showed her birthmark. No longer was it a brown splodge but a little silvery cloud. Poppy smiled and admired her new birthmark.

Although they were both stood in a dark, empty space, they could see each other clearly, and there was a warm feeling around them.

Poppy ran into her mother's arms, holding on tightly around her waist, never wanting to let go.

'Oh Mum, I love you,' she said through sobs.

'Poppy, you're beautiful. You're my beautiful little girl. I've missed you growing up. I've missed making you happy, and I've missed telling you off for the bad things you do. But I'm here now, and I know I can't make up for it. But I'm here for now for all that matters,' she whispered, also crying now.

'Mum, oh Mum, I can't even remember hugging you. I'm so glad I can.' Poppy shut her eyes tight and took in a deep breath, like the breath she took when she past the bakers, but this time, she couldn't smell freshly baked bread; she could smell her mother's clean clothes and her sweet perfume.

Poppy and her mother spoke all night. Poppy explained how she was now a fairy and was to become a queen. She told her how she came across the house, the book, Sophia, her grandmother passing away, and how she was terrified of becoming a queen.

Her mother listened, content, overjoyed that she could finally talk to her daughter like other mothers did. She told Poppy why she was living in heaven. She told her about the evil, life-taking demon called cancer and how she died soon after Poppy was one. She told her how her grandmother had it, and the only thing keeping her alive was the book and Poppy. Once she had found the book, she could make sure Poppy could be looked after and then peacefully passed away. Both Poppy and her mother cried when they spoke about this.

Poppy began to tell her mother about Yasmina and Amelia, but her mother just smiled and said, 'I know, Poppy, Yasmina can summon me to her dreams too. We are still good friends, and she has told me about you and Amelia's friendship, too. But now I have to go. I'll be back. All you have to do is thinking of me as you fall asleep.'

And with that, her mother faded away, and Poppy was waking up in her big, comfy armchair.

Chapter Seventeen

Royal Life

Weeks passed, and although many thought it was impossible, the prince and Poppy fell in love even more. They learnt each other's secrets, they knew everything about each other, they knew all the little stuff like Poppy's favourite ice cream flavor was strawberry and the prince hated apple juice and coincidently Sophia's favourite as well. The prince's father, King Alexander the fourth, had died fighting for Dreamland, which he won, and the prince was saddened because he had died before seeing the land he earned. Poppy told the prince how her mother and father were divorced, a thing no one knew of in Dreamland, and as she did, the prince took her hands in his and promised her they would never make the same mistake her parents did. They would lie for hours under the sun near the lake near the edge of Dreamland or under the big oak tree in the palace gardens and never get tired of each other's company, and they laughed and talked all through the day and most of the evening.

Poppy saw her mother most nights in her dreams, and they talked like they were best friends, not mother and daughter. One night, Poppy fell asleep clutching her best pencil and her mother's book. And in her dreams, her mother flicked through the pages, slowly and carefully, just like the way Poppy did the very first time she saw the book. She saw tears in her mother's eyes as she saw the pictures, so she held out her pencil to her mother.

'Draw me, please, Mum.' She grinned.

And without a second thought, her mother crossed her legs, putting the book in between them, opening it, and placed the lead on to the paper. Poppy sat up straight and smiled at her mother who concentrated on her daughter's perfect cheekbones, wavy shoulder-length hair, slightly pouted lips, and large round, sparkly eyes. She blinked away tears as she sketched away, and before she knew it, she was awake, clutching her mother's book.

She sat up in bed and propped herself up on a pillow and looked at the hard, pink, and slightly glittery cover of the book. She opened up the first page carefully and looked in amazement again at the queen's beauty like she did the very first time she saw her. She carefully turned the page and saw her future husband's handsome loving face; as she looked down, her stomach turned in a funny way like there were little butterflies fluttering around in her tummy. She saw the words 'My husband' written underneath. She flicked over the page and saw the picture of Yasmina, and turning the page again, there was the picture of her mother when she was younger, but the annotation this time read 'My mother as a child.' She realised that her mother had not only added Poppy's picture, but put it up to date. She saw the picture her mother had drawn of Poppy, and underneath it said 'Me.' She closed the book and turned to the back, and instead of the old, scratchy writing on the back, there was a new note stuck to the back in her mother's handwriting, the same as the annotations in the book.

The note read: 'Dear Poppy, this book is now yours. I hope you take good care of it and pass it on to your children. Only the very, very special people you love very much can go in here as it's a very special book. That's why you are in it now. Love you forever, Poppy, from Mum. XXX'

Poppy smiled and jumped up and out of bed. She skipped happily into the next room and slid the book into place on the bookcase and after getting dressed into a silky, navy blue blouse and thin jeans. She placed her feet into some black ankle boots, and after brushing through her hair and teeing it up, she headed out and down the cobbled path.

As she passed the bakers, she took the usual deep breath and carried on walking before stopping in her tracks. She turned on her heels and held her head high and entered the shop.

Her eyes widened the way they always did as she approached the counter of cakes, buns, and loafs of bread. The whole shop seemed to have a golden glow.

She suddenly felt so young again, the way she did when her grandmother would take her to the sweet shop. She wanted to pick everything up and take it home.

She smiled at the baker, a small, fat fairy, whom she recognized from the announcement, known for flying about with his family.

'Hello, sir. Do you have any iced buns, please?' she asked politely.

'I do, your highness. How many would you like?' he answered, smiling broadly.

Poppy froze. 'Sorry, what did you call me?' she questioned.

'Err your highness,' said the baker, confused now.

'Ah, yes, that's what people will be calling me now, isn't it? Um, I'll just have two please.' She smiled. She had forgotten how different life would be now when she was to marry the prince.

The baker carefully chose a bun with pink icing on top, and on top of this icing, he placed a big, glossy red cherry. He put it into a box and handed it to Poppy.

'They were made fresh this morning. You will enjoy that, your highness,' he spoke.

'Aha, thank you, sir. I'm sure I will. How much is that please?'

'Fifty pence, please,' he asked, holding out a rather fat hand.

After Poppy had paid, she flew up the cobbled path and crossed it until she reached the school.

She walked through the gates and across the playground, in which every little boy and girl fairy stopped skipping, running, dancing, playing catch or football and just stood, staring at the princess who had just entered the playground for the first time. As Poppy looked around in search, she remembered how much fun school used to be and how fun the freedom to play whatever you liked in the playground.

All of a sudden, Amelia ran up to Poppy and gave her a huge hug.

'Hello, Amelia!' laughed Poppy, hugging her friend back.

'Hi, Poppy! Why are you here?' asked Amelia.

'Well, I just thought you might like a treat for lunch today,' said Poppy, handing over the box.

'Wow! From the bakery? Thank you, Poppy! I'll see you soon,' cried Amelia, running off to show her friends what the princess of Dreamland had just bought her as Poppy left through the gates of the playground.

Poppy spent the rest of the day at the castle with the prince. When she arrived, the prince sat next to the stone pillar that held up the gate, and he was talking to the guard and was propped up on one arm. As soon as the guard saw Poppy, he bowed and opened the gates for her. As she stepped through the gap between the huge black iron gates, the prince stood up and took Poppy by the waist, the way he did the first time, and kissed her lips. His kisses never got old; every time she saw fireworks. There wasn't a moment with the prince that Poppy didn't have fireworks or butterflies.

Hand in hand, they strolled through the gardens, over little stone bridges, above a little stream that ran through the whole palace gardens, full of golden and silver fish. They flew through a wooden gate at the back of the palace. The gate led in to another little garden surrounded in stone walls, covered in ivy. To Poppy's surprise, the whole ground was carpeted with beautiful red rose petals. There wasn't a touch of grass or soil in sight, just red rose petals. It was the perfect little sun spot that glowed with warmth. There were stone features dotted around, of different fairy characters, adding to the beauty of the garden. Two big comfy-looking armchairs were in the middle with a small table and parasol in between them. It wasn't much, but to Poppy, it was so romantic, and she thought it was the perfect way to spend the day.

'It's beautiful.' Gasped Poppy.

'My father created this place for him and my mother. They never came in here though, because they never had chance. My father died before he had a chance, and mother won't enter here without him. So I thought it could be ours,' said the prince, putting his arm around Poppy's waist and kissing her cheek.

Poppy cautiously stepped on to the petals inside the gate, and to her surprise, they didn't move or crumple but still felt as soft roses underneath her feet.

'They're magic, in case, you're wondering,' said the prince. 'They will never ruin, crumple, or die.'

Poppy smiled and walked in. She felt the sun hit her and caught her golden wings sparkling in the sunlight. She rose into the air, the prince joined her and took her hands, and they began to dance wonderfully together.

'You know, we should probably start planning our wedding,' said the prince as he took her hands.

'What's the rush? We're only young, Alex. We have our whole lives ahead of us!' smiled Poppy.

'Don't you want to get married? We have been engaged for nearly a year and a half,' he said, doubtfully.

'And I'm only just sixteen! Of course, I do. I just like us like this. Getting married doesn't make us any different, and I'm not sure I'm ready to be queen just yet!'

'You will be a perfect queen. Don't worry about that. All right, there is no rush, so don't worry about that either. I just want you to know I love you! So much!' he said as she leant in and kissed his cheek.

Poppy's heart leapt with every step they took in sync, and their eyes didn't leave each other's. They laughed and flew through the air happily, never wanting it to end, but after a while of dancing, they floated back down on to the carpet and lay on their backs with their eyes closed and stayed that way for most of the day.

'How old were you when you had your first kiss?' Poppy asked her mother that night as they sat talking in her dream.

'About sixteen. I would never kiss anyone until I knew that they were the one. My first and my last kiss was your father,' said her mother, combing through Poppy's hair with her fingers gently as she spoke.

'Last? But didn't you divorce?' asked Poppy in some state of confusion.

'Yes, we were. After you were born, things got so stressful. We were always fighting, so we decided it would be better to live separately. Then when I had cancer, he was there with me the whole way. He never left my side, and we realised we were so stupid for cracking under the pressure. We thought we weren't strong enough to get through it all, but we were. And as I lay dying, I held you in my arms, and he kissed me goodbye,' said her mother. Now she had stopped combing through her hair and was wiping away tears falling from her eyes.

'If you realised that you loved each other again, but it was too late, why did I live with my grandmother and hardly see my father?' asked Poppy, also wiping away her tears now.

'I had to make sure you found the fairies, of course. I told him he had to trust me, and he said that he couldn't watch you grow up without him from afar, so he told me as soon as my funeral was over, he was moving to the Caribbean,' spoke her mother.

'The Caribbean? That's a bit random.' Laughed Poppy through tear-filled eyes.

'Your father always loved the sun. He always seemed to be tanned. Anyway, why did you ask me how old I was? Have you kissed the prince?' asked her mother, wanting to change subject before she began to cry again.

'Of course, I have, Mum! I'm to be his wife! But even though I know with all my heart it's right, I can't help feeling so young!' said Poppy.

'What makes you say that?' said her mother.

'Well, I'm almost seventeen, and I know I love the prince. I went to the school today to see Amelia, and it just felt like I should be there, not planning a wedding!'

'There's no rush to get married, Poppy. That won't change the way that you feel about the prince,' her mother said, going back to combing through Poppy's hair.

'I know that. I even told him that today. I just, I really don't know how I feel right now,' cried Poppy.

'You're a clever girl, Poppy. Follow your heart. Only true love can last in Dreamland. And yours and the prince's has lasted, so don't worry, please, my angel,' said her mother, before kissing her daughter's forehead and fading away softly.

Poppy awoke in her bed, happy that she had spoken to her mother again and happier that she felt she had a clearer head now. Her mother had helped her.

Chapter Eighteen

The Wedding

After months of planning, those running through Christmas, in which everyone spent at the palace, the queen, the maids, and other servants, the prince, Poppy, Amelia, and Yasmina all sat down to a grand meal of melon, turkey, potatoes, carrots, peas, and gravy and then ate marvelous chocolate cake for afters. Poppy had spent weeks, gathering everyone presents and choosing just the right thing.

For Amelia, she made a little dress, a cream one that was loose and flew down to her knees. She made her a matching woolen cardigan and bought a cream headband that had a flower on it from one of the stalls in the market place. When she was buying the headband, she spotted a little blue teddy that looked soft and cuddly; she picked this up too and gave it to Amelia at Christmas. Amelia jumped for joy when she opened her parcel Poppy had so carefully wrapped. She hugged Poppy tight.

'You really are the best friend ever, Poppy. This dress is amazing, and I'll call my new favourite teddy Poppy,' cried Amelia.

For Yasmina, she had got her a big box of different flavoured teas as she had learnt Yasmina drank a lot of tea when she was working, so Poppy thought this was a nice idea. There was green tea, red berry tea, herbal tea, lemon tea, apple tea, mango tea, cinnamon tea, mint tea, and many more. Yasmina grinned at her parcel when she had opened it and simply said, 'You're too good at choosing perfect presents, Poppy!'

The prince has specifically asked Poppy not to get him a Christmas gift and said he would be sad if she did, so she just handed him a card and gave him a big hug and a kiss as they all sat around the fireplace in pyjamas watching the snow fall from the window.

Amelia handed Poppy an envelope.

'What's this, Amelia?' questioned Poppy.

'My Christmas present for you, silly,' said Amelia, urging her to open it.

Poppy opened the envelope, and inside was a piece of paper, folded up, tiny and was shoved into the corner of the envelope. Poppy opened the piece of paper several times until it was full size and saw that Amelia had drawn her picture of Poppy and Amelia holding hands; they were surrounded by flowers, and in each spare hand, they were both holding a pink iced bun with a cherry on top.

'Thank you!' cried Poppy with a tear in her eye. 'I will frame this, and put it on my bedroom wall,' she said, hugging Amelia.

'I've got one too,' said Yasmina, cutting in and handing Poppy a small pink parcel.

Poppy tore of the paper excitedly with a big grin on her face as the prince put his arm around her to get a closer look at the present. Poppy held a little glass bottle in her hand; it was a pink bottle but slightly transparent. She could see that inside there was some sort of cloudy liquid, so she took of the lid and sniffed the inside.

'You made me some rose perfume! Thank you so much, Yasmina,' she said, carefully placing the bottle down and hugging Yasmina.

They planned their wedding down to every last detail until, finally, a warm day in June; it was the day.

Poppy woke in her palace bedroom as she had stayed the night before with a tight grip on a little silver box and a pair of shoes. She knew straight away why she had; her mother had given them to her that night in her dream. Poppy soon realised that she had woken to Lucy flying about in her room. She opened the curtains on her bed and put down a tray on the side Poppy was not lay on.

'Your breakfast, your highness. You must eat earlier today. Are you excited?' she said after curtsying and going back to opening the window curtains.

Poppy got up and put the shoes and box on to her dressing table and then climbed back into bed, propping herself up on her pillows.

'Thank you! I am, Lucy. Oh, banana flakes! My favourite! How did you know?' she asked, tucking in.

'I didn't, miss. You haven't forgotten about the magic of Dreamland, have you?' said Lucy, heading for the door.

'Ah, yes, I must have fancied them when I saw the bowl of cereal. Thank you, Lucy. Are you coming today?' Poppy asked, through a mouthful of banana flakes.

'Certainly, miss!' exclaimed Lucy before flying out of the room.

Once Poppy had finished her breakfast, she began to get ready; she washed and then went over to the wardrobe to get out her dress.

She had made her dress herself, the way she wanted too. It was a wonderful, white corseted at the top with Victorian laced flowers in the front and a crises crossed lace up back. The dress spread out on top of a dress hoop at the bottom in many layers. She straightened out her wings she was so proud of and stepped into some small shoes, the ones her mother had given her last night in her dream. They were her mother's wedding shoes and had a slight heel and a band of little white roses going across the top of the foot. She sat down at her dressing table and combed through her hair; in the corner of her dressing table was a silver box her mother had given her in her dream. She was told sternly not to open it till now, so when Poppy saw it sat there, she couldn't wait to open it. She placed the box in the palm of her hand and opened the lid gently. Inside was a very thin gold chain, and as Poppy lifted it out, she saw that there was a little golden heart dangling from the chain. She put it around her ankle and realised why her mother had said, 'If you know what to do with the contents of the box, I will be with you every step of the way through that wedding.'

Poppy smiled at the thought of her mother being close to her now and continued to get ready. She straightened out the teddy bear necklace around her neck.

She looked at her hair; *something was missing.*

She opened the door a little and peered outside. No one!

She opened the door wider and stepped into the hallway. She ran across quickly until she came to the room with the balcony. She peered inside, again, no one! She went inside and shut the door behind her. The table was set for about twenty people who would have meal after the wedding. The room was beautifully decorated in pink and white, their wedding theme. She pulled back the thin curtain covering the window and opened the door, stepping on to the balcony silently; she took up the view and tried not to be noticed by the finely dressed guests who were entering the castle. The whole village had decorated the streets and their shop windows with flowers and buntings to celebrate the royal wedding. Posh-looking cars were parked outside the castle, and all kinds of magical creatures were coming: fairies, hobgoblins, pixies, trolls, gnomes, elves, and water and flower fairies. Poppy went over to the edge of the balcony and leant over. She could just about reach the flower boxes below; she picked out some small white roses, clutching them in her hand. She left the room as it was and snuck back into her room.

Just as Poppy had finished pining up her hair and putting the little white roses in-between locks of her curly, long blonde hair, the fairy queen knocked at the door.

She entered in a long, white dress with flowers all the way down the side, a dress Poppy had never seen the queen wear before as she always wore big gowns. She had a glamorous white hat on her tied-up hair.

'Lovely dress, miss,' said Poppy, smiling at the queen's beauty.

'And yours is too,' said the queen, now smiling back at Poppy.

'Thank you. Do I look okay?' Poppy asked, standing up from her dressing table stool and standing up straight. She had decided against make-up for this occasion because for her wedding, she wanted to look natural.

'You look like a queen,' said the queen herself, putting down a veil and a small golden tiara on her head.

'Thank you,' gushed Poppy.

'Well, are you ready?' asked the queen, indicating that it was time.

'Yes, I think I am,' said Poppy in a whisper, spraying on a little of Yasmina's rose perfume.

They both headed down the stairs that had been decorated with white ribbons to where there were a number of maids and servants waiting. They all gasped as the nearly new queen carefully stepped into the hall. And a big 'wow' came from a little girl stood behind them all.

'Hello, Amelia. You look lovely,' said Poppy as Amelia stepped into view holding hands with her mother. They were both dressed in a pale pink dress with puffed sleeves and a shawl, and they both held a bouquet of pink and white roses.

Poppy could hear music coming from the throne room and people chattering. She knew that was where her future husband was waiting to marry her. She stood before the door, and the queen handed her a large trailing bouquet of pink orchids wrapped in a white ribbon and linked arms with her.

The doors opened, and loud, slow music started as every fairy and magical creatures Poppy had once dreamed of and read about in story books stood up from their chairs, and they entered the room. Poppy and the queen walked up the aisle, and from behind her veil, Poppy's eyes darted around the room, a huge smile upon her face. The prince turned around, hands behind his back and smiled at his beautiful bride. His eyes were fixed to hers, and they didn't move until she had reached the altar. He was enchanted by her beauty and graciousness.

In front of Poppy, also in matching pink dresses, April and May threw a carpet of pink rose petals for the queen and Poppy to walk on. Behind Poppy, Amelia and Yasmina had hold of her dress train, and behind them, a line of maids and servants followed and took their seats. Even

Rike and Moss had tidied themselves up. Poppy could feel her mother beside her as she whispered from behind her veil.

'Mum, Mum,' she said repeatedly until she was sure her mother was with her on her special day, the way it should be on any girl's wedding.

As Poppy reached the altar, she pulled back her veil daintily, and the queen, April, May, Poppy, and Yasmina stepped away into their seats.

'You're beautiful,' whispered the prince before the fairy vicar began to speak.

After saying 'I do' and the prince's cousin Henry passing the rings to them, they slid the gold bands on to each other's fingers, and the prince kissed the bride. They were there again, like always; fireworks blew around in their heads as they kissed, and everyone clapped and cheered.

'We did it!' cried Poppy, turning around to see all her friends clapping for them, and for a moment, somewhere in the back, Poppy saw her mother, grandmother, and grandfather, all smiling at the back, but when she blinked, they were gone. But she knew they were there and was so happy she could share it with them.

Later that night, the prince and his wife sat on their thrones after their wonderful meal of roast chicken as their grand ball began. All the fairies were wearing ball gowns and posh suits, and Amelia came and hugged her best friend as Yasmina was dancing with Henry, and as they caught sight of each other, Poppy winked at Yasmina whose faced turned a bright red colour.

Poppy stood up from her throne and began to dance with Amelia to her favourite song. She was so happy; she never wanted the night to end. Amelia giggled and smiled as she danced, but suddenly, some hands were around her waist, pulling her away from the princess as the song changed to a slower tune.

'Come on, dance with Mummy!' said Yasmina, starting to dance with Amelia.

But Poppy wasn't standing alone in the hall for long as the prince bowed to the princess, and she curtsied before they took each other's hands; everyone cleared to the side of the hall as they began to dance to their wedding song. After a while, the other fairies joined in, and they all danced right through the night.

Chapter Nineteen

Becoming Queen

The newly married couple loved life together; they moved into the palace for a while, but Poppy felt bad for leaving her home empty, so they moved there together. They often had dinner parties and friends around and spent all their time together. No one would think they were royalty; they lived and were treated like normal people, the way they wanted it.

Finally, the day had arrived for the queen to retire. She couldn't wait; she wanted to relax now and so was happy she could hand over her crown at last.

It happened on the balcony where the wedding announcement was made. Poppy and the prince sat whilst trumpets blared and hundreds of fairies watched in silence. The queen took off her crown and walked over to Poppy, who sat nervously looking at all her friends below. The queen carefully took off the tiara from her head and held the crown above.

The trumpets stopped, and the queen spoke out confidently, 'I, Karena Garner, the queen of Dreamland, crown you, princess Poppy

Garner, the queen of Dreamland and I accept to retire.' She placed the crown on her head.

The queen finished by turning to the crowd and saying, 'I give you the king and queen of Dreamland,' before letting the king and queen stand, hand in hand, before the now cheering crowd. Again that night in the palace, there was a grand ball, and Karena asked Poppy what she would like to wish for.

'Wish for? Why do I have a wish?' asked Poppy, confused.

'Every new queen gets a wish,' cried Karena.

'Oh, I didn't know that,' said Poppy, thinking hard. 'I know what I'd like. May I whisper it to you?'

'Anything for the queen.' Giggled Karena.

So Poppy whispered her wish to her husband's mother, and the queen smiled and took out her wand, which she waved in the air.

'There, done.' Smiled Karena.

'Nothing's happened?' said the king.

'Oh, it will!' Smiled the queen and Karena together.

Karena handed Poppy her wand.

'Now this is yours. Don't misuse it,' said Karena.

Poppy thanked the queen and promised only to use it when she needed and put it away.

The same night, it was agreed Karena would retire to Poppy's little home and Alex and Poppy would live in the palace as king and queen.

'Can you believe it?' said Poppy to the king as they watched fairies dance and laugh together, especially Henry and Yasmina, but Yasmina always swore they were just good friends, and it's perfectly normal for good friends to spend as much time as they do together. But everyone knew they were more than friends as Yasmina had confessed her love for him to Poppy's mother when she met her in her dreams.

'I can believe anything now, Poppy. But what I believe most is that I love you, and I always will,' said the prince, leaning in to kiss his wife.

'I love you, too! I've gone from girl to dressmaker, to princess, to wife, and to queen, all in just a year. But I don't want to change anything now. I'm so happy, Alex!' Poppy said before hugging him.

Chapter Twenty

Wishes Coming True

Yasmina and Henry married sometime later, just like everyone had said, and Amelia grew to be a beautiful young lady. Poppy still saw her mother every night in her dreams, and when she was twenty-eight, she had a beautiful baby girl with big, sparkling blue eyes and blonde curls. The day she was born, Poppy smiled and said, 'This literally is a dream come true.'

The king's mouth made a huge 'O' shape as he realised the night Poppy was crowned, and she made a wish. Now finally it had come true. Poppy and the prince knew as soon as they saw their baby that her name was to be special. So that night, as their friends came to visit, Poppy held her baby in front of her best friend and said, 'Amelia. This is Amy.'

Now when Poppy looked through her big pink fairy book, it was full of all the special people in her life, and none of them would ever leave the pages, because they would never stop being special to her, and she had an everlasting love for them, especially her husband, King Alexander, the fifth.

I would say 'THE END' like any good story ends with. But this story is only just beginning, and if I were to continue with this story, I would be here for a very long time.

CPSIA information can be obtained at www.ICGtesting.com
Printed in the USA
BVOW071433150312

285292BV00001B/116/P